NEW WORLDS! NEW ADVENTURE!

Published in Canada by Engen Books, St. John's, NL.

ISBN-13: 978-1-989473-71-9

Distributed by:
Engen Books
www.engenbooks.com
submissions@engenbooks.com

First mass market paperback printing: September 2020

Cover Design: Vaughn Marsh

Slipstreamers Committee:
Amanda Labonté
Ali House
AJ Ryan
Ellen Curtis
Erin Vance
Lauralana Dunne
Matthew LeDrew

NEW WORLDS! NEW ADVENTURE!

MATTHEW LEDREW & JD RYOT

CHAPTER ONE

Cassidy slammed chest first into the stone ledge, letting out both a long gust of air and a curse so strong she wouldn't have said it on any continent that her mother might have been in. She paused briefly before gravity began to take hold, tugging at her quickly and dragging her down towards the gaping maw below.

She dug her nails into the crevasses of the stone, sliding until she found purchase and ground to a firm halt, her nails pulling against their beds and threatening to break. She turned, red hair whipping and clinging to her sweat-laden face as she looked down the embankment she dangled from.

Intellectually, she knew that no pit was bottomless. But when her feet kicked and dangled over a chasm so deep and dark that it disappeared beyond her focal point, it was hard to find any other word for it.

The walls around her began to shake and vibrate. Dust and silt that fell between them, making a distant rumbling that she knew was coming closer with every passing second. She ground her teeth together and pulled, her jacket protecting her from the coarseness of the stone as she pulled her body back onto solid ground.

Behind her, the ledge she'd leapt from cracked in two with the shifting of the temple's foundations. It stayed that way for a moment, as through the split would be the worst of it, before several quick jolts made it snap apart and fall into the abyss below.

She let out a long, deep breath and laid on her back before bringing her right hand up into her field of vision. She still clasped the lead disk she had taken from the tomb, the small ringlets along its edge spread between her fingers. There was a square hole in its center, through which she could only just see the gash that had been sliced through her palm. Despite the pain that ebbed from it, she smiled as she looked at the artifact.

"At least I've got my tetanus shot," she smirked.

The ground beneath her moved and she laid her hands flat to steady herself. As if on cue a large, lightning-bolt shaped crack opened in the stone beneath her, splitting from the mouth of the cavern to the ledge she'd just crawled over. She turned quickly, scrambling onto her feet as dust and sand kicked loose. She bolted for the exit, slipping twice on loose grains before finally making it out into the humid air of the Nubian sun. She gasped as the cloud of dust followed her, outrunning it as the temple door slammed shut behind her.

"Are you okay?" her Guide, David, said, running over to her. He laid his hands on her shoulders and she laughed: a full, honest laugh. He took out a pouch of water and handed it to her. She leaned back her head and doused herself with it, revealing the freckles that had been hidden under the dirt and grime of the enclosure.

She drank from the skin and handed it back to him, then turned over and pressed the pointer and middle finger of her right hand into her neck. "Come on..." she huffed, still stifling her laughter. "Come on..."

"What're you--" David started. She held up a finger to stop him.

"Sixty-four, sixty-five... sixty-six." She paused, waiting. "Sixty-six." She cursed. She looked down at her hands, ignoring the slice along the right palm and spreading her fingers wide. She turned her palms down and then up, examining them as if waiting for them to do something.

Cassidy cursed again, then rose to her feet and started the long trek back to her camp. David followed close behind.

***

"And that's how I retrieved the Amulet of Ra, one of the ten fabled Amulets of the Ok'Tid," Cassidy said as the lights came up and the projector wound down. The absence of the bright light made the lecture hall visible, with all two hundred seats of it filled with students and still more standing along the back wall.

She smiled with showmanship, turning and spreading her arms towards the iron disk, which now rested comfortably in a glass display case. She felt like Vanna White while doing it, her smile wide and forced, pushing her cheeks up so far that they obscured her vision.

"Once thought to be a myth, this relic was believed to be a part of a set that, when combined together, possessed the ability to make their wielder *immortal*." She turned and stepped closer to the case, the fake smile fading. She tugged at the edges of her coat, the same brown leather she'd been wearing in the temple, but now clean, until it fit around her shoulders properly. "This legend stems from the region, going as far back as three *thousand* B.C., and is thought to be one of the precursors to modern healing myths. Your fountains of youth, your holy grails." She turned sharply on her heel and pointed to the case, her fingers clicking like a gun. "It all starts right there, and until last month we thought it was lost to time."

Several of the students in the front row leaned forward, as if trying to get closer -- if only by a few inches -- to the artifact. To Cassidy's right, near her entrance to the hall, came a loud cough. There were four men standing in the door -- three large and one much older and shorter.

Cassidy nodded, turning to address them. "And it is of course being handed over, with appreciation, to the Plainsfield Museum, who have agreed to fund the Archeology and Anthropology departments for a further three years." She brought her hands together to lead the applause, and most of the students followed. She did so gingerly: her hand had healed, but a pink line of tender flesh remained.

The men stepped forward until they flanked the display case. It looked at first as though they were about to step forward and speak, but instead they turned their backs to the student body. Two of the larger men picked the case up off of its podium, and the lot of them walked back the way they'd come with it.

Cassidy coughed, and her feigned smile returned. She clicked a button on her remote and the projector whirred back to life, displaying an image of the amulet on the screen behind her. "Were there any questions?"

Fully half of the students present raised their hands immediately.

She smiled and pointed to a tall blonde girl in the third row. "Yes?"

"I guess the thing I have to ask, it sounds silly... but with all that going on, weren't you scared?"

Cassidy paused. She looked down at her hand, splayed out with her fingers wide, not shaking in the slightest. When she looked back up again she had resumed her public smile: that broad, too-wide and too-bright expression she put on for others. "I must have been, mustn't I?"

CHAPTER TWO

"That," Cassidy said, making a big circle with her red pen on the page of text in front of her, "is not how a preposition works."

The stack of papers in front of her was large and oppressive, a tower that shifted and swayed whenever the air conditioner kicked in. Which was often. They teetered near a framed photograph of an older couple and two young women: the photo was old, but the frame was new.

Her office was small and cluttered, only six feet across but a full ten feet long, with the door at one end and her desk on the other, near a window that barely opened but let in the heat of the sun all throughout the day.

The space between the door and the desk was packed tight, so tight that she had to squeeze and maneuver to make it through. There was a wide wooden chair of the sort that came with any University office, she felt. Against either wall was a bookshelf stacked with reference materials, most of which now gathered dust -- a byproduct of a digital age. Atop the stacks of books and along the ridge of each shelf were trinkets -- artifacts from different regions that hadn't been needed by the University or the museum. There was a fat doll made from hollow wooden balls and catgut. There was a plate gold-plated disk with a hollow center and small shards of shimmering metal dangling from it.

Stacked beside the bookshelf against the west wall was a box overflowing with maps, each of which looked well used. Several were on the floor around it, and one was spread over a corner of her desk like a tarp, a days-old yet full cup of coffee weighing it down. Next to the box of maps was a large globe, upon which all the landmasses were a light tan color and the oceans were a deep, chocolate brown.

Cassidy found that she'd been staring at a spot on the globe with the sort of trance-like boredom that she sometimes found herself doing -- especially when correcting papers. The place she was staring at was deep in the center of Mexico, a section of Mesoamerica she'd marked long ago with four red stickers she'd never been able to remove. She forced herself to look away from them and back to the work in front of her. "And that is a comma splice connecting a faulty argument," she said aloud, circling the splice and then striking out the problematic sentence.

She sighed.

On the page, the words began to blur and jumble, and before she knew it her head had lolled up towards those red stickers on the globe again. She sighed again, then reached over the stack of papers and gripped the map that hung over the edge of her desk. She inched it forward until the coffee cup was in reach, then picked up both cup and map and brought them down in front of her. She took a long sip of the ice-cold liquid, slurping it as she spread the map out over the essay she was correcting. She took her red pen -- no longer for correcting -- and marked a spot quite near the center of Mexico.

"It's the boredom, isn't it?" came a firm, hoarse voice.

She looked up from her map and saw a man standing in her doorway, his heels in the hall and his toes firmly in her space. He was a short, portly man in a suit that looked expensive but hadn't been fitted properly, a sign of a man who had money but hadn't had it long. He had a smattering of incidental facial hair and was balding, with glasses so thick they were what her grandfather's generation would have called 'Coke Bottles.' They rested atop a small nose and a kind, wry smile that traveled up one side of his face. Despite the fact that Cassidy was sure she'd never seen the man before, he still looked familiar.

"Pardon?" she asked, straightening a little. She wasn't sure yet if he was even entering the room. Some people -- especially men of a certain age, she'd found -- thought of open office doors as an excuse to step in and make a comment. It was typically a comment that the speaker considered to be in good humour, regardless of the fact that nobody ever laughed.

"The boredom. It all seems good, it seems like maybe this time you'll be able to stay... catch up on your office hours, maybe binge the latest season of that show that's on your DVR... but the moment you sit down, the boredom hits. And suddenly it all feels the same, and the office feels too small." He stepped in on the word 'office', looking around at the books that lined the walls. "Quaint."

"Is there something I can help you with?"

"Yes, I dare say so." He turned to one of the shelves, examining a long row of volumes on Papua New Guinea with his hands clasped behind his back.

Cassidy waited a long, pregnant moment for a further response. "And that is?" she said finally.

He smiled, almost unknowingly. "I need help with my latest project. The project is... well it's your cup of tea, actually." He turned to her. "I need your help finding a cure, for more than just boredom."

He said the word *cure* with the U sound drawn out, inflecting up at the end as though he were saying the word *demure*. It was slight, but enough that it triggered a dormant part of her memory. "Are you..." she paused, glancing at the photo on her desk again, at the only male in it. He was smiling with broad, full cheeks. The man in the photo was not the man that stood before her, but one had saved the other, even though they'd never met. "You're Dr. Gamgee."

He grinned. "Herbert."

"You cured McMillon disease." Her cheeks were flushed with warmth.

"And, potentially: boredom." He smirked, running a finger along her books and coming back with a thick layer of dust on the digit.

She stared for a moment, then forced a smile. "I just got back from Nubia. Brought back one of the ten Amulets of the Ok'Tid. It's priceless. Literally, without price. Once in a lifetime discovery. History book stuff. I'm not..." she paused, leaning in and smiling for dramatic effect, *"bored."*

He turned to her and smiled that knowing smile. It was

the sort of smile people had when they'd known you your entire life and could see the culmination of everything in your every statement. "Then I suppose your pulse got up above seventy beats per minute?"

She opened her mouth to answer before she'd really processed the statement. Once she'd heard it she stopped short, her finger hanging in the air.

He nodded. "Join me for a meal. I hear your cafeteria is horrible." He turned and stepped out of the room without looking to see if she was following.

She narrowed her eyes, watching him go until he was out of sight. Finally she cursed, pinned the map back to her desk with the still-full coffee mug, then grabbed her coat.

CHAPTER THREE

The cafeteria at Plainsfield University was wide and open, with the sort of flat white tiles that used to be only found at cell phone carrier storefronts, but had in the years since been utilized anywhere that desired to look modern. False glass walls divided and herded the traffic from the kitchen, lined with USB outlets and creating a false sense of privacy while still making everyone visible.

Gamgee took a bite of his taco. Lettuce fell from its lower half onto his plate, tumbling out like water over a falls. He laughed at it, trying to catch it at first and then giving up. As he swallowed he said, "It's been years since I had one of these."

Cassidy squinted at him from across the small, round table. She had a plate of fries in front of her that was largely untouched, a healthy smear of spicy ketchup next to the mound. All around them students moved and shifted, bustling from tables to classrooms and back again. Her vision was locked on the man who sat before her in an ill-fitting suit, letting everyone else move in and out of her peripherals.

"You cured McMillon disease," she said finally and

declaratively.

He paused, let his head warble from side to side, then nodded.

"You are one of the world's most celebrated medical doctors, so I feel like I owe you the time here. But I didn't come to talk about tacos. So let's get to the point before I get--"

"Bored?" he smirked.

She lowered her eyes at him. "*Distracted*."

He nodded empathetically, wiping his mouth with a paper napkin. "Physicist, actually," he corrected, waggling a large finger at her.

She raised an eyebrow. "Pardon?"

"You said I was a world renowned medical doctor. I never got my MD. I'm a physicist, world renowned for an advance in medical science." He took a long drink from his soda through a straw.

Her eyebrows scrunched together, but she said nothing.

"But I understand. You're a busy person, I'm a busy person," he took another sip of his drink, "we all have places to be, so I'll approach my point. Or attempt to." He took the salt and pepper shakers from the edge of the table and pushed them closer to the center, between Cassidy and him. He paused, laid his hands flat on the table, then looked at her. "Do you know what McMillon disease does?"

"I know the effects."

"Yes, but how does it do that? McMillon disease affects the... oh, I can never remember the term. The *garbage collector* genes. Things build up in our bodies, our lymph tissue, on our nerves, etcetera. Your body has functions that remove that gunk and let it pass."

Cassidy nodded.

"McMillon disease inhibits those functions. The gunk builds up on the nerves and synaptic fibers, and things get... things get bad. Slowly, in stages. Sometimes in stages so slowly that people don't realize it's happening. Most people know it for the loss of the senses." He took another bite of his taco. "That gunk, it builds up on the nerves around the eyes and around nerve endings... people lose their sight, their touch sensitivity, their hearing... everything."

Cassidy's right hand touched the finger on her left uncomfortably, before she forced them apart again.

"In the end it mimics Alzheimer's, but by then with McMillon... well, by that point with McMillon most of the sufferers have already died, if we're being honest."

She nodded.

"It's an awful disease. Truly. So ten years ago I found a treatment, which I turned into a cure." He sipped his drink. It was nearing the bottom of the cup and made a slurping sound through the straw. "That's the thing that people don't get: McMillon disease isn't something you get, it's not HIV. You're born with it. It might stay dormant or inactive, but if it was going to activate in you it's going to activate. No amount of healthy living or good life choices will circumvent it. It's genetic." He shrugged with one shoulder. "So apart from gene therapy, which we don't yet have for it, there's not strictly a 'cure.'" He used air quotes when he said the last word.

Cassidy shifted uncomfortably, her gaze shifting

around the room briefly.

"There's just the treatment. You treat McMillon disease, and eventually with rigorous treatment the affects can reverse. In the best of cases it can reverse totally, to the point that the treatment is no longer necessary on a daily or even monthly basis... but the underlying cause, it's still there." He took the pepper shaker from the table and held it up at eye level, like a token. "But you know how some people are." He moved the shaker to the other end of the table, then gestured at it. "People don't take their prescriptions as doctors prescribe, and doctors don't take human behavior into account. All around, people are dumb. They take their treatment until they feel better, or until they can't afford it or..." he shrugged. "Any number of reasons. But the point is they don't take it as instructed. So the gunk builds up again, but in new ways. *Resistant* ways. It builds up on some nerve types more than others."

He tapped the pepper shaker on its head. "So now we've started to see McMillon disease Stage Two."

Cassidy felt gooseflesh break out across her arms in one long wave.

"Stage Two is... different. You don't see the same sort of nerve damage to the senses. That still gets managed with treatment. Where you see it worst is cognitive function. The gunk, it starts to line the nerves in the brain. And once it starts there, it's hard to get at. The treatment, it doesn't chip away at it like it does the nerve endings outside the brain."

"What does it do?" she asked, her voice hurried.

"It causes degradation of brainwave activity. Some in

the field liken it to Alzheimer's, but honestly as we learn more and more about Alzheimer's... the comparison is less and less apt. But, broad strokes, sure." He paused, wetting his lips. "Not many are to that point yet, but we're starting to see it. The early signs actually resemble split brain patients."

She furrowed her brow.

He brought all his fingers up to the middle of his head. "There's this bundle of nerves called the corpus callosum that connect the right and left sides of the brain. We used to sever it in seizure patients... we don't anymore, don't worry. But those that did -- split brain patients -- whoo man, you'd see wild things. You see the left hand arguing with the right about what snack to pick up, or what shirt to wear. The left hand will just... reach out, and slap the right hand choice away." He paused. "It happens because the left brain is mute. It usually communicates across the corpus callosum, but when that's severed it has to communicate in different ways." He sipped his drink. "It's deeply distressing."

Cassidy nodded.

"As McMillon disease Stage Two progresses, there's more and more gunk on the corpus callosum, to the point that it hinders communication. So we start seeing behavior like split brain patients. Benign stuff at first... clutter on one side of a desk but not the other. The left hand picking up things to answer a question and then the right-brain controlled mouth making up a reason why it's holding it. Over time... over time this gets worse. Eventually there's nothing to be done."

There was a long pause between them, where all that

could be heard was the gentle sway of the crowd moving to and from their classes.

She swallowed. "What does this have to do with me?"

"The treatment -- Duplionyl -- it doesn't work for Stage Two. Or it works, but it just doesn't work on the most destructive elements." He paused, taking a deep breath. "I never told anyone how I found the cure."

She squinted. "No. But then... aside from penicillin, how many medicines do we know the story behind?"

He waggled his finger at her again and smiled: a big, toothy, honest smile. His teeth were too far apart, a slight gap between each one. "Quite right. I think that's why it's never been questioned, not really. But now we're here and we need the cure for Stage Two... and I'm too old to get it."

She straightened. "Get it?"

He smiled. "Let's just say... there was more to finding the treatment than leaving some bread out to get mouldy. Like I said, not just a cure for McMillon... but for boredom, too."

"Why me?"

Gamgee looked at her for a long, slow minute. "You're Dr. Cassidy Cane. *The*. It honestly didn't take a lot of research."

She fidgeted again. "I'm in the middle of planning a new expedition right now. I can't just get up and--"

"You're correcting papers and thinking about maybe going to Mexico for the fourth time before something else sidetracks you, and you go do that instead. Before you chase that buzz." He said this with less levity than he'd spoken with up to this point, his voice becoming serious. "That feeling, that excitement... when you can feel your pulse throb, not just in your neck but in your earlobes. In your fingertips. That big, defining surge of excitement."

She stiffened, her back ramrod straight and her elbows cocked at ninety-degree angles.

"That feeling, I guarantee, you will not find in Mexico."

"I have to go," she said, standing up from the table. "I have papers to correct."

He frowned, then nodded and dismissed her with a wave of his hand. She turned without saying goodbye, making a bee-line away from him to the hall that led back to her office. When she was gone, he reached over and touched her plate of fries, sliding it across the table until it was in front of him.

***

Cassidy returned to her office, her face flushed and tinged with green. She made her way to her desk to resume correcting her papers, then stopped and pushed them to one side. She closed her eyes and took several long, deep breaths, then opened them.

The old photo in the new frame was directly in front of her. She tisked and picked it up, tracing first the edge of the glass, and then the familiar lines of the man's face. She pursed her lips, then fished her cell phone out of her pocket.

"Hello, Mom?" she said when there was an answer. She forced a smile: you could hear a smile over the phone, she'd been told. "Yes... yeah I am back, actually. A week or so now." She ran her fingers through her hair, gripping her scalp. "No... sorry no, I've been busy. Yeah... so hey, I was wondering..." She looked back at the photograph on the desk. "I was wondering if I could come over for a meal."

CHAPTER FOUR

"Can you pass the mash turnip?" Preston Cane asked, holding his hand out with the palm up and fingers splayed, ready to receive the bowl. Cassidy smiled. Her father's idiolect was something that had never ceased to bring warmth to her face. The way he said 'mash turnip' instead of 'mashed turnip,' 'Chicargo' instead of 'Chicago,' or any number of other small inflections that were uniquely him, always brought a fresh grin to her face.

She raised the blue swirled bowl of mashed turnip high as though it were a prince she was presenting to the Pridelands, then set it down with great weight on his waiting hand.

He laughed.

The dining room of her childhood home shrank more and more every time she returned to it, to the point that she wasn't sure if she'd be able to get out to go to the washroom without asking her sister Margo to scootch in. Even then she would have bumped her shoulder-blades along the edges of the vinyl paintings that lined either side of the room, threatening to crash them to the floor and eliciting a series of disgruntled tisks and rasps of air from her mother.

Her mother, Kayla, sat at the far end of the table, eating edamame that had been drizzled in olive oil and topped with fresh black pepper. Every time she bit into one Cassidy could hear it across the table, even above the chatter and laughter of her sisters, Margo and Rica.

Margo was twenty and had been a theatre arts student at the local community college for the last year. She'd been Margaret all her life up until she'd graduated high school, but upon coming home from that first day of college she'd been asked to set the table by her given name and had corrected them with one spinning, erect finger: "Actually, it's Margo now I think." She said it in such a way that she had expected it to be questioned and was ready to start something over it. It hadn't been. Cassidy and her parents had just shrugged, gotten the carrots ready, and asked *Margo* to set the table.

Rica was a year younger and had always been Rica, as far as she could remember. Whenever her full name, Frederica, was said over the loudspeaker at school, it always took her a moment to realize they were talking to her. It was a name that sounded foreign to her ear, despite being technically hers. Rica was the more quiet of the two. She hadn't graduated yet, but was planning on attending Plainsfield University when she did, and had politely asked Cassidy not to put herself into the process, one way or the other. Cassidy had respected that, as had their father, when she'd told him.

Her father finished scooping the mash turnip, which was now a hefty mound on the right side of his plate. He put the bowl back onto the table in front of him, then picked up the gravy boat and added a healthy dollop to the pile, turning it into a volcano just as he had when they were little. She had thought at the time that it had been just for their benefit, but it was clear now that it was not.

"Eruption on mount turnip," he said under his breath, his grayed eyebrows high and exaggerated.

Cassidy and Rica laughed, more at the memory of the joke than at the joke itself.

Across the table from him, her mother smiled wanly, then took a long sip of her wine. "How long did you say you'd been back, dear?"

Cassidy turned, as if suddenly realizing there were more people in the room than just she and her father, and pushed her hair back behind her ear. "A little over a week," she said, then took a bite from her pork roast. After a moment of eyeing the sheen on the cutlery, she forced herself to return her mother's steadfast gaze. "Sorry I didn't call to tell you."

Her mother smiled naturally and shrugged. "You're a grown woman, Cass. You don't need to tell me every time you come into the country." She paused, letting her grin slide up over her cheeks after a scant moment. "Did you bring back anything with you?"

All parties at the table turned to Cassidy at the question. Margo wiped sauce from her mouth.

Cassidy grinned. "There was this ah... yeah, there was this thing." She grinned, laying down her fork so that she could talk with both of her hands. They formed a loose sphere in front of her, as though she were trying to conjure whatever she was talking about. "This Amulet... thing." She laughed. "Until a few years ago everyone kind of assumed it was a legend, but I kept seeing this circle in different texts and glyphs and stuff. This symbol, at the end of a lot of really portentous and pretentious religious and cultural texts." She smirked. "This one guy out of Cambridge, he'd found references to it that he thought meant it was punctuation, like a really emphatic form of a Full Stop," she laughed.

"And it wasn't, I assume?" her father egged warmly, poking her elbow with his own.

"No, yeah... no. I mean I see why he thought it was. He kept seeing it as this reference to 'everything ending with this'. Like a sentence, or a paragraph. Just one of those 'you have taken this too literally' moments." She took a sip of her water. "And I was looking at it and I realized it was a thing. Like it wasn't a concept, it was a visual representation of a thing. A thing that ends everything."

Margo raised an eyebrow.

"It doesn't really," Cassidy laughed, waving off the implied criticism with some jazz hands. "But when we kept digging I found these ancient texts and references, remnants from a bunch of different cultures. Like some sort of original template for all the end of times myths we have today. And it was these Amulets, the ten of them. And so I followed the patterns and, well..." she shrugged, leaning back on her chair. "I found one."

"Nice," Rica nodded. Cassidy lifted her hand as if to say it was nothing.

Her mother hummed in agreement from the opposite end of the table. "Was it valuable?"

Cassidy cocked an eyebrow and looked sidelong at her mother. "It was thousands of years old. Possibly one of the original devices used to tell stories, ever. I had to fish the thing out of a temple that was rigged to crumble if it was removed from the place, which it did. Like something out of an old adventure serial or something," she drawled.

"Is that a yes or a no?" she asked, as though Cassidy had said what she'd said without emphasis.

"It's *priceless*, mother," she said finally, putting both her palms face up in the air in front of her, as if displaying a large tray of money.

"I think what your mother wants to know is," Preston smirked. "Is it priceless as in expensive, or priceless as in worthless?" He shoveled the last of his mash turnip into his mouth when he was done his dad-joke.

Cassidy laughed. "The department is funding me for a further three years off of it."

"Oh darling, that's fantastic," her mother smiled. She lifted her wine glass to toast her, then took a long sip.

"Yes, wonderful," her father returned, clasping his weighty hand on her shoulder and patting it heartily.

Her smirk faded, and she picked up her fork again, the gleam of it catching her eye as she looked back down. "You're right," she said, forcing a smile. "It's fantastic."

Preston clapped her once more, laughing proudly. "That's really great, Cass. Really. Can you pass the mash turnip?"

Cassidy raised an eyebrow at the repeated request, but picked up the bowl and handed it to him, this time without humour. He took it graciously and started pulling more and more orange mush from its depths. When he was done he put the bowl back where she'd gotten it from, just to his left and well within his reach.

"Thank you," he said, smiling sincerely.

"You're welcome," she returned. "You must really love Mom's mash turnip. They must be your favorite."

"They are," he smiled, his left hand picking up his fork and plucking a carrot with its spears. "I can't get enough of them. I'm sorry, has everyone else had enough?" He looked down and switched the utensil from his left to right hand, ate the carrot quickly, then resumed scooping up his mash turnip.

"I'm fine," she smiled, almost blushing. She narrowed her eyes, and when she spoke again it was with trepidation. "Would you say they're your favorite though? The best ever vegetable?"

"Hands down," he laughed, as though the question itself were laughable. "It's the brown sugar, gives it this extra zing." He picked up his dessert fork in his left hand, plunged it into a carrot again, then switched both to his right hand.

She cocked her head towards the bright orange root vegetable. "Why do you keep doing that?"

He paused, then looked down at the fork in his hand. After a moment he smiled. "Well you haven't had enough, clearly. Kayla, are there any more carrots in the kitchen for Cass to have?"

"I'm good, thanks," Cassidy said, raising her hand politely. She took a deep breath that nonetheless failed to fill her. She stood from the table. "I have to visit the restroom, if I can be excused?"

Margo scootched in to let her pass.

***

Cassidy stepped from the restroom into the crowded main hall of her childhood home, still wiping her hands on her pant legs. She heard her family downstairs, still laughing over something her father had said, their voices already seeming unreal and far away. She swallowed, then made her way down the hall, away from them.

She passed her former bedroom without looking into it, closing the ajar door as she passed. When she reached the end of the hall she turned and entered her father's study, either side of it occupied by a bookshelf piled high with texts, just like her own. Unlike hers, his office was wider and much less claustrophobic. Also unlike hers, his books were well read and never had the chance to form dust. Most were paperbacks, and they were either kept and reread often or donated to goodwill, but they never stayed in one place for very long.

His desk was cluttered, as hers had been. But rather than covering the entire desk, it was confined to the left side. The right was clean, undisturbed, and reflecting the light from the window back at her.

On the shelf next to her was a picture of she and her father on a fishing trip, many years ago. He leaned over her and she into him, pressed cheek to freckled cheek. Their hats had hooks on them that they never used, and they were getting tangled in one another. There was a man on her arm opposite her father with a square jaw and kind eyes, smiling right along with them and holding a large bass.

She looked behind her, into the hallway and then,

swallowing hard, stepped around the desk and moved her father's seat out of the way. She opened the second drawer down without looking and reached inside, pulling out an orange prescription bottle. The label across it read 'Duplionyl' in its cold, sans serif font. The dosage period was from well over a year before, but she could see five pills still rattling around in the bottom of the bottle.

When she looked, there were seven other bottles in the drawer.

She cursed, bringing her hand up to rub her furrowed brow.

CHAPTER FIVE

Herbert Gamgee's lab was a warehouse with a walkway that went all around it, spreading into smaller offices that could be occupied by other people in the field, but weren't. The space was wide and open, cold both in temperature and emotionality, the light off the stainless steel instruments giving it an unearthly clean glow. It had been used for testing deep sea equipment at one point. He'd bought it once the site was decommissioned and used it to house his work.

Echoes were a constant fact of life in the space, so although he heard Cassidy Cane enter the building long before she reached him, he'd made no effort to put down his newspaper and address her until she was within ten feet of him. When she was, he lowered one corner of his paper and looked up at her, his face sallow and without expression.

"The cure to the next stage of McMillon disease," she said breathlessly. "I'll help you find it."

He nodded, taking his feet down off of a mini-fridge that was marked with a biohazard sticker on one side. "You changed your mind fairly quickly."

"Yes well... I went home and looked up how many people suffered from it. You can't just do nothing, in the face of that many."

He eyed her for a moment, then smiled. He stood up and walked with her to a large table on an adjacent platform. It had a dozen seats around it, each one bathed in a blue hue from above that disguised the fact that they were black leather. When he reached the opposite end as her there was a keyboard waiting, the cord of which connected to a small bobble in the center of the table. He pressed four buttons and the bobble began to glow blue, and before she realized what was happening his computer screen appeared as a hologram hovering above the desk before them.

She was taken aback for a moment, then smiled.

With two more clicks, a map of Plainsfield, Massachusetts faded into view.

"Did you ever wonder how a physicist cured a biological problem?" Gamgee asked, eyeing her mischievously from between the glowing lines of the map as he zoomed in further. The University retreated to the side as the map continued to zoom into the coast.

She watched him for a tense moment, then shook her head.

"I thought not," he tisked. "No one does, really. I had a whole story planned, a whole thing. I never once got the chance to use it. I blame the media. Whenever there's a scientist character on a team, they just have them be good at science. In general. All fields." He laughed, then turned back to her. "Does that happen in your field? People expect you to know about every culture? Every historical period?"

She smiled and nodded. "Yes."

He bobbed his head. "I thought as much. Good to know it happens to everyone." When the map had zoomed in so much that it focused only on the state's rocky coast, he pushed both his hands to the right. The screen responded by shoving the entire map away. What was left was a blinking blue cursor in the middle of a star-field. He moved his hands forward and small dots appeared, corresponding to each of his fingers... then he stopped. "How to explain this."

She squinted.

He drew two glowing blue circles in the air, one with each hand. "Have you ever heard of the Mandela effect?"

She shook her head. "I've heard of Nelson Mandela, is that--?"

"Yes. Well no, but: yes." He smiled, waggling his finger at her again. "Nelson Mandela was a prominent political figure up until his death in the mid 2010s... and yet there are some who vividly remember reports of him dying in the 80s. Hundreds of people, in fact. Tens of hundreds." He smiled, perfecting the edges on the circles he'd drawn. "And there are yet more oddities. The spelling of a popular children's author's name. Different versions of movies that have come out. Deaths that didn't happen, others that did. Slight variations on reality." He paused. "It led some to postulate that they'd come from another world."

Cassidy laughed, bringing her hand to her face to quash it.

Gamgee looked back at her from between the two circles, without humor.

"You can't be serious," she said, letting her hand fall to her side.

With one quick motion he pushed the two circles together, making a Venn diagram of them. At the points where the two diagrams intersected, they glowed red. "Imagine two worlds, two *dimensions* stacked on top of one another, nearly identical save for a few small changes. And over time, those changes grow and diverge."

"The Butterfly Effect."

"*Exactly*. But in this, both can coexist. Both matter. But there still remain... links between them." At the world 'links' he motioned to the red dots, and they began to blink a soft, ephemeral hue. "Spots in reality indistinguishable to the naked eye, but if one should stumble through one, they would find themselves in another world. Likely without even realizing it."

Cassidy squinted. "Without realizing it?"

Gamgee nodded. "Unless the traveler looked for the differences, they would have no clue. None. They might even come back, if they hit the same spot in just the same way, by chance. Imagine it: people able to walk in and out of reality with the ease of air flowing in and out of an open window." He smiled broadly, pushing his cheeks back and showing all his teeth. His glasses glowed blue in the light from the projection. "Now imagine if you knew where that doorway was."

He swiped both hands to the left, minimizing the diagram of the two circles and returning to the map of the Massachusetts shoreline. Now, in one small spot along the bluffs, was a red oval dot blinking with a soft, ephemeral hue.

"That's where I discovered the cure," he said, his voice now almost a whisper.

Cassidy stared at the blinking red oval, and for the first time in what felt like years, she felt the heat of her pulse rise into her cheeks.

CHAPTER SIX

"There may be some disorientation when you step through," Gamgee said as he navigated his way past a large, smooth boulder.

Cassidy stopped in her tracks just a little down the slope from him, turning to him with narrowed eyes that pushed her freckles up towards the crest of her nose. "You said people managed to walk through this and not even realize it." She paused. "You said that people could step through this thing into another world and not even realize what they'd done -- that they'd just keep living their lives and think the changes were lapses on their part."

"And that's true. For most."

They were five miles from the outer edge of Plainsfield, in an area populated by dense evergreen trees and brush that continued to the very edge of the continent before suddenly dropping off into large, tanned boulders. They came together haphazardly and yet with great purpose, laid there like toys a toddler was done playing with and yet firmly in place after an age of time and pressure. They formed caves that dotted the shoreline, lined with kelp and small shellfish. The tide was out, but it was clear that at another day or time the caves might have been hip deep with crashing waves.

She continued to squint up at him, the late evening sun behind him making him into a dark silhouette. Without thinking about what she was doing, her hand drifted to the pouch on her hip. She unclasped its button and let it hang open like that, ready. "I'm warning you, if this is a con, you will live to regret it."

"There's no con," he said. His Adam's apple bobbed when he said it, descending to the furthest pit of his throat before rebounding to the middle. It stayed there, quivering in the cool air coming off the water.

She narrowed her eyes more, then turned and continued down the embankment, along the path he'd marked. She kept her pouch unbuttoned. "Watch your step."

They came off the steep boulders onto the relative flatness of the shore, a brief edge of ten feet that bordered the last edge of her world before disappearing into the oblivion of the sea. The waves were such a deep blue they were nearly black, like ink pushing its way towards the unspent parchment of the forest. They crashed and rolled, leaving creamy foam in the crevices and cracks of the stone.

She turned back towards Gamgee as he finished his decent. His back no longer against the sky, he came out from the silhouette he'd been in and seemed the kind, portly man again: less sinister by circumstance. Behind him the trees were thick and black with the shadows of evening, but she scanned their expanse with a weather eye she'd trained over many, many years of action.

Unexpectedly, they found a bear walking along the edge of a steep ridge of the cliff, its fur barely visible between the trees but clearly there all the same. It ate berries the way only a bear could, entire branches of the bush finding their way into its mouth and then being strained through clenched, sharpened teeth when it pulled back. It ignored them, far enough away that neither party was a danger to the other. It was used to humans. Even this far into the wild, there was no wilderness.

She sighed, then turned her attention to the caves and parts of the rock face they'd scaled down. They were slices in the cliffside, holes that came to sharp points at the top and bottom, widening into foot-long gaps at their middles. They gaped like maws, small breaks in reality where light had no place. There were several of them in varying shapes and sizes, some appearing more inhabitable by an adult human form than others.

"Which one were you talking about?" Cassidy asked, looking from one to another with a tense, analyzing gaze. Her eye found a mark along the right side of one, a set of two identically-curved squiggly lines that were nested into one another, spooning. She tilted her head.

Gamgee moved to stand alongside her, his head roughly adjacent to her squared shoulders, and surveyed the same cracks in the wall that she did, as though he'd not been the one whose instructions led them here. He waited, not making a sound or gesture, letting her continue to scan the ice-flow remnants.

"It's not that one," she said with decisiveness, gesturing towards the cave with the squiggles carved next to it. "You're trying to keep it hidden. So..." she trailed, letting her eyes fall over it again. The lines were slanted right and she followed their path to a gap in the rocks that was elevated slightly above the rest, wide at its bottom and curving dramatically at its peak. With imagination, it looked like a wizard's hat. "It's that one," she said finally and with certainty.

"Very good," he smiled, nodding. He started towards the break in the rocks she'd motioned towards. "Symbology is something that must come in handy for someone in your line of work."

"It has its moments."

"It will have many more, I think," he smiled.

Again, she squinted at him.

They reached the edge of the cave in near unison. Now that they were closer the black depths looked less black, with some light filtering in from the setting sun. She took out her phone and activated its flashlight with several deft, familiar motions of her thumb, illuminating the cave in iridescence. It was deep and damp, the sides slick with condensation and castoff from the sea. It was too narrow for Gamgee to fit into by half, and barely wide enough to squeeze even her hips through.

"Homey," she said under her breath, even as her light caught something shimmering and reflective along the cave's curved interior peak. Her eyebrows came together as she moved the light to see it better, revealing a small shaft of metal, no wider than a tube of lipstick. Her nose crumpled as she turned her light to fault points in the rock on the left and right sides of the cavern, and then finally at the lowest edge as well. She turned back to Gamgee. "Nice try, but--"

"They're explosive, be wary of them," he admitted, gesturing to the metal items.

She stopped mid sentence.

"It's dangerous, I know. But as I said, these doors work both ways. Never too careful." He looked down the length of the cave as he spoke, as if expecting something to be waiting for him in the dark of it.

She squinted at him, then turned her gaze to the cavern. "It's empty."

"If it were glowing blue, everyone would find it." He almost laughed. "Look again."

She scanned the interior of the cave again, trying hard to not focus on the metal shafts that kept attracting her attention, as dangerous and obvious as they were. The shimmer of the walls reflected back at her and the very back of the cave could not be viewed, but other than that there was... "Nothing," she said. "There's nothing."

Gamgee tisked. "You disappoint me," he smiled, without disappointment. He took her phone from her gently, then aimed it at the rock floor. A small stream of water trickled from it, down past their feet and out towards the sea.

She watched it go, finding its way down the stone shore and generating the same cream-colored froth as the sea as it tumbled. "It's a stream. All running water heads towards sea-level... if I'm meant to be impressed by something, I'm not."

"Look at where it comes from."

Cassidy sighed, then took her phone back and aimed it towards the cave's wall, looking for the split in the stone the water was produced from... and found none. She frowned, shining the light down at the stream and then following it back to a large piece of stone a foot into the cave, where the water appeared from the stone's midpoint, as if from nowhere.

She tilted her head curiously, then smiled. "I've lived on this coast my entire life. A stream can seem to come from nowhere, but there's always a source of--"

"Taste it then," he said, his voice devoid of all humour for the first time since they'd exited his vehicle.

She paused, then leaned down and cupped her hand under one of the water's crests. It took a moment to fill to her knuckle, then she brought her hand to her lips and sucked back. She spit immediately, cursing.

Gamgee laughed.

"Salt!" she said, still sputtering. "Salt water."

"Where it should be fresh," Gamgee said, bending to squat and watch the water that flowed, as if from nowhere, from the rock in the cave. "The tide is different there. Low here when it's high there, and vice versa. The water, it just laps at the edges of the portal when it's at high tide... a little bit of our world into theirs, a little of theirs into ours, with every push and pull of the tide."

Her eyes widened, and without doing it consciously, she backed up from the cave a single step. She reached for her thermos, took a long glug from it, swished it around her mouth, then spit it onto the rocks below to get rid of the last of the saline taste. She repeated this twice more until the taste was gone. "This is impossible," she said finally.

"I recall saying the same thing when I first found it," he nodded. He was still watching the salt water from another world as it trickled down over the rocks, past his feet and into the sea. When his voice returned it was wistful and faraway. "Years looking for a thing, trying to prove it exists, only to find it and your first thought be to deny it." He smiled wryly to himself, pressed his hands to his knees, and pushed himself up. "We're odd, aren't we? Humans?"

She nodded, glaring not at Gamgee for the first time but past him, into the dark of the cave. She said nothing. She straightened, arched her back, then stepped forward until she was at the mouth of the cave again. She shone her light in one last time, turned it off, then turned and handed it to him. "I don't suppose there's cell service there."

He smiled. "None that we'd pick up, anyway."

She nodded, gently pushing her head and shoulder into the cavern.

"As I said, you may feel disoriented," Gamgee reiterated, tucking her phone into his pocket. "I find once you think you're through you feel the need to breathe in, but it's actually better to exhale. But don't hold your breath stepping through, you want to--"

Gamgee's voice cut short in mid syllable, and a sharp snap of pain erupted from the back of Cassidy's head. The mouth of the cave became blurred suddenly.

Cassidy lost consciousness with his words ringing in her ears.

CHAPTER SEVEN

Cassidy woke up with salt water splashing on her face. It was light at first, but was then accompanied by a roar and splashed down on her with force. She jolted upwards, coughing, her hair clinging to her neck and cheeks in fiery red clumps. She gasped, then cursed.

Above her, she could see metal shafts embedded in the rock face, sputtering blue sparks and illuminating the cave. She cursed again, rising to her feet and bolting through the mouth of the cave. She found herself shin deep in salt water, the tide trying to pull her back towards the sea. She turned and fought it, making her way back up onto dry slate before catching her breath.

She cursed again, so loud and with such vulgarity that she was almost glad no one was around to have heard it. After a moment to catch herself, she felt for her keys in her pouch and located them. She sighed with relief. "He best not have hotwired my car," she fumed, even as she began to pull herself up over the ridge. "Never should have trusted that little madman."

She pulled herself up onto the ledge by the tufts of grass that grew there, the midday light warm on her neck as she ascended. Even when she reached the top, there was no one in sight. She sighed, then started to make her way west towards the start of the treeline.

***

Her car, just as she'd worried, had been missing.

She had been walking the Massachusetts back highway for almost three hours, feeling the oppressive heat of the sun on her neck and shoulders the entire time. She hadn't packed her sunscreen, she'd realized after the first hour. She hadn't packed for travel, a rookie mistake she chided herself for, and not Gamgee. She had her water, but it was running low.

Sweat billowed down over her freckled cheeks. She'd considered retreating into the shade of the forest on several occasions, but the memory of the black bear she'd seen on the bluffs reminded her every time that she'd left unprepared for danger.

"Stupid," she said to herself, though her tongue was a dry slug in the center of her mouth. "Of all the stupid things to believe. He probably knew about your father... wasn't he in the town paper last year, for the fundraiser? And every time there's a Birthday Charity on social media, you give to McMillon disease. Every time. Doesn't take a genius."

She huffed. "You are a stupid, stupid person sometimes, Cassidy Cane."

Behind her, far in the distance, she heard the soft drone of an engine.

At first her brow furrowed, thinking it was Gamgee returning in her car to end his great prank. Then her brow softened: it could be help. It could, in fact, be anything. She turned and raised her arms high into the air as she did, ready to flag down the (hopefully) Good Samaritan.

There was nothing on the road.

But still, the sound grew.

She furrowed her brow again, slowly lowering her hands as she stared out upon the hilly, dry landscape she'd just hiked over. There was no movement save for the dust and grass in the breeze. She waited to see if the car was hidden in one of the dips and valleys she'd come over, but even after waiting longer than should have been needed, there was nothing. And yet still, the engine whir increased.

Her hair began to flutter, even despite being weighed down with perspiration, and dust began to swirl in clouds around her as the sound became louder. She looked up and saw it at last: the long, rectangular body of a car, travelling past her and over the embankment at high speed. When it flew overhead the gust was such that it almost pushed her down, and from within she heard screams and yelps of praise.

Red streaks followed in its wake, caught in the vapor trails left by the vehicle's passing and slowly ebbing out of sight.

She covered her mouth to block the sand, trying to catch her breath as she watched it disappear over the peak of the hill. "What in the world?" she gasped, bolting forward with new energy. She climbed and climbed despite her arches aching, finally mounting the summit of the blind hill.

There was a city in the valley, where there had never

been any such city before. In all her travels, she'd never seen a city anything like it. Blue and green skyscrapers lifted into the sky, so high that they pierced the clouds, coming to sharp points. Their windows shimmered against the sun, each one shining natural light back at her. The tallest building was dark blue with a symbol at its apex, a red man with a white cross on its belly.

Cassidy's eyes went wider still as she saw the flying cars -- not just the one she'd seen, but *dozens* -- making their way in and out of the city. There were no suburbs, just skyscrapers that travelled for miles and miles, and yet she saw no hint of smog or pollution. It looked like it had grown out of the landscape, like deep forest trees that had been alive longer than man and rose up to heights that boggled the mind. It shimmered and glowed, casting off so much heat that it had a mirage effect on the air around it.

She found the strength to swallow, then continued down the highway towards it.

CHAPTER EIGHT

As large as the skyscrapers had seemed in the distance, they were much, much more so when standing among them. Cassidy had spent a month in Dubai last year on an expedition, and had stood at the very foot of the Burj Khalifa and stared straight up its mass. It might have been merely situational, but she thought it now paled in comparison even to the average of these towers.

She bumped shoulders with people who didn't obey the laws of traffic. There didn't seem to be laws of traffic here: no right lane forward, left lane back. Somewhere in the back of her mind, she wondered if that was a consequence of perfecting flying cars: rules of the road ceased to be the law of the land. She tried to adjust but found it impossible, and so tried to avoid getting within arm's reach of anyone.

Despite the height and cluster of the buildings, somehow she still felt the heat of sunlight. She squinted up at the buildings, and saw that their edges were lined with what she would have called retroreflectors, but weren't, that shone the sun's rays down to street level. "Clever," she said to herself.

Behind her, several heads cocked suddenly at the sound of her voice and watched her as she continued down the street.

There were no street signs, but the buildings were alternating shades of blue and green, and never quite the same shade twice. The greens were getting lighter the more blocks she walked, she noticed, and the blues lighter. She remembered the presentation Gamgee had given about the divergent timelines and wondered just how far back the timelines would have had to have diverged to make it so that street signs had never been thought of, and instead color coordination used. *A hundred and seventy years at least,* she thought, struggling to remember her history. *Unless they had them once and have since outgrown them?* That detail change, although small and benign, seemed incomprehensible. She tried to remind herself that she'd thought the same about foreign cultures on her own world on some of her early expeditions, and that this alternate Earth was under no burden to be more familiar than her own.

I wonder if they even call it Earth?

She passed by a blue region into one of aquatic green, where there were canopies hanging from the edges of the tower, each with its one symbol on it. She did not recognize them, but each had the plump silhouette of a man with a different symbol somewhere on his body. Many were on his stomach, at least the majority, she estimated.

Steam wafted into the air from under the canopies, sending smells foreign and yet familiar churning towards her nostrils: food. Suddenly she remembered how hungry she was from her journey and started to look from side to side. She knew where she was suddenly, the cultural differences melting away as the rose-colored glasses of her point of view finally faded: she was in a market.

There was a grill that let out hot hisses of steam as she walked by, a motor rotating what she would have called beef kabobs along its edge. The fruit on it was charred strawberry and pierced fresh lime, a strange combination she'd never heard of and yet, in many ways, could not wait to try. The man serving it had a long mustache, of the sort she associated with travelling salesmen from the wild west. His apron was made of denim and he held onto the straps proudly as he surveyed for customers, only furthering the association. She stifled a rude laugh, not wanting to offend in this strange place, and quickly stepped away from the booth.

There were five women wearing what looked to be shaylas, but the edge framing their faces was bright gold and the main fabric was a bold, dark red. They stood out against the greens and blues of the architecture. They carried pouches of dried fruit in their hands that they'd bought from the vendor behind them, and were trying to get the young children that ran around their legs to ingest some. One, the one closest to Cassidy, was holding dried peaches out in front of herself and making a series of cooing noises, as though trying to coax an animal to do what she wanted. Cassidy thought at first glance that they had been family, but realized now that there was not a common trait between them: not hair colour, eye colour, body type, face shape... not even tone of flesh. They spoke a language she couldn't recognize -- and she recognized many -- that to her ears was made of too many vowels and hard

Rs. She had trouble distinguishing where one word ended and the next began.

The woman selling the dried fruit smiled at her with her arms wide, and Cassidy smiled back. There were many vats of dried goods -- most of which Cassidy recognized at a glance -- each with its own plastic shovel wedged into it, and she recognized it as a kind of portable bulk depot.

The next booth had a man and a woman behind it. Each wore solid colors -- one green and one blue -- and stood with their hands behind their backs like military personnel awaiting orders. Their faces were expressionless, yet menacing, and their eyes seemed to watch Cassidy as she passed. They were armed. They were the first weapons she'd seen since entering the city limits.

The table in front of them was lined with pill bottles, almost exactly like the ones she'd found in her father's drawer, right down to the child-proof cap. The only difference that she could see was that instead of orange, this world's bottles came in sharp greens.

The pills inside even looked the same. There was writing on the bottle in a language she couldn't understand, but there was also a symbol like the one she'd seen on the building from the horizon: the outline of a plump male figure in red with a white cross on his stomach.

She lingered by the table for a moment, then looked to the attendants -- who were looking back at her -- and then to their weapons. They continued to stare at her.

In front of the pills were pamphlets, though hexagonal and oddly shaped, with the same white-crossed man symbol on it. She took one and held it up to them, nodding politely. They did the same, a regimented motion, not a social one.

She moved on quickly.

The next three stations sold prepackaged tubes of fried meat, and the proprietors talked among themselves as if they knew each other quite well. She couldn't follow the conversation they were having, although their language seemed different from the one she'd heard the women using. There were still too many vowels, but the hard R sounds had been replaced by elongated Ks. Even their laughs sounded like Ks, and they laughed often. Even without context, Cassidy could recognize people engaging in locker-room talk, by the body language and laughter, if nothing else.

One of the men was emptying pills from a green bottle into his hand, even while laughing with his friends. He took out an imprecise amount and popped them into his mouth mid sentence, and the other two showed no signs that this was odd behavior.

Cassidy moved on the the next vendor, a tall woman with purple hair and a broad smile selling hot sandwiches. They were pork and Cassidy could smell what must have been horseradish swirling up from them, and salivated. She made eye contact with the vendor and smiled, only noticing at the last moment the top of a green pill bottle sticking up out of her breast pocket.

Cassidy's smile fell. She turned back to the street she'd come down, now looking for something specific.

There's no way... she thought, even as she scanned the crowd. Several shoppers had pill bottles in their hands, the green plastic color showing through their fingers. Others had bulges in their pants pockets, the right size and shape to be them. Still more were stopped at the pill vendor, purchasing them in varying stages of a transaction.

The man with the large mustache and denim apron had a bottle peeking out his front pocket.

As she watched, the woman in the dark red shayla that had been coaxing a child forward with a dried peach was now wedging a small pill into the flesh of the peach, feeding it to the child, and patting him on the head.

Cassidy stammered, unable to speak, and almost tripped as she turned back to the sandwich cart. She forced a smile at the vendor, who smiled back. She sighed. Each of the sandwiches rested on thick squares of parchment paper that one was clearly meant to wrap around it to hold. She plunked her finger down on the largest of them and slid it forward, the smell from it somehow intensifying as she did.

She reached into her pouch and began to withdraw her compass. "Look, I'm sorry I can't pay at this exact moment--"

Behind her an old woman's head spun towards the source of her voice, and her formerly relaxed gaze devolved into a hateful scowl. She let out several hard R words with very few vowels in them, each word having a distinctive bite and single-syllable cadence to them. A man near her -- her son, perhaps -- tried to coax her away but looked back with the same darkened expression.

The purple-haired woman behind the booth, whose smile had been so sweet before, had changed her expression to one with a slackened jaw and wide eyes. Her cheeks had even lost some of their color. She opened her mouth to speak, and from her lips came a series of soft vowels that Cassidy could not tell from each other, strung together with hard R sounds.

"You don't speak English," Cassidy sighed, nodding. "Of course you don't. Why would you? That's... that's silly of me, really."

The purple-haired woman leaned in, her teeth bared and hands outstretched. It was the motion an adult did when trying to stop a child from touching something hot.

Cassidy squinted, then slowly turned her head. She no longer had to force a bubble of personal space around herself in the crowd: the crowd was providing it all on their own. She swallowed, then lowered her voice and extended her hand with the compass in it. "Listen I'm... I'm hungry, okay? I need food. This is gold. I hope... I hope that's worth something here. If you could just--" She reached out for the woman's hand to place it in. The woman pulled away.

Cassidy sighed, then lay the compass down on the table roughly and slid it forward. "Thank you," she drawled under her breath, taking the sandwich off the table.

Several other vendors called after her as she left, a volley of hard R and long K sounds following her until she turned the corner and escaped the market square. The purple-haired girl did not call after her: she picked up the compass with the same amount of awe and reverence as Cassidy had had when she'd found her first artifact.

CHAPTER NINE

Cassidy sat on a small concrete ledge near the mouth of an alley, five streets removed from where she'd parted with her compass. The blue buildings were darker here, and the reflective strips on the side of each was less and less effective and bringing the sunlight down to street level as a result. She ate the last of her pork sandwich, the wax paper crinkling and popping as she brought it to her face.

The pork had been infused with the horseradish somehow. It had been pickled with it in layers, and the flavor combination -- though surprising -- was strangely magnificent. The best of it by far had been the bread. She didn't think she'd ever tasted bread so soft and so warm, and it had remained so even now, right to its last bite. It fell apart in her mouth like butter.

She chewed the last of it absently, staring out past the frame of the alley into the street beyond. She was well past the market now, and into an area she could only have assumed was a business district. Men and women walked back and forth on the street wearing suits that were similar enough to the ones she remembered, except that they were always in exacting shades of green and blue. There were several different shades, like the buildings, but only so many. They walked and talked on cell phones and smiled and cursed and laughed, all in that same too-many-vowels language she'd heard back in the crowded market. As much as she tried, she still couldn't ascertain where one word ended and the next began without an obvious, emphatic tell.

It was like watching people pantomime western behavior. Like AIs stepping from one fixed point on a map to the other, each time yammering gibberish that she tried not to think of as such.

A green suited man with an extreme widow's peak of black hair stopped at the corner. He took an equally green bottle of pills out of his pocket and poured them into the cup of his hand. He separated two, dry swallowed them, then pushed the rest back into the bottle. He straightened his shirt, stood up straight, and stepped back into the chaotic pace of traffic as though it were nothing.

Across the street there was a woman in a red gown that stood out from the rest, walking slowly among the crowd. She carried a small pail of change with her and a sign -- which was written in an alphabet that Cassidy was also completely unfamiliar with -- affixed to it. She didn't appear to be derelict or in need. *Collecting donations for a religion, maybe,* Cassidy thought, her eyes following the woman as she passed. She spoke little and had a sweet smile, the ways nuns on her world often had.

How far back must this world's divergence point be that we aren't on a Latin-inspired alphabet? she wondered, as the sign and its holder faded from view. *At least 400, but prob-*

ably more. Probably far, far more now that I think on it. That is, assuming I'm not on a part of this globe where my alphabet just isn't in use.

Across the street, a sallow woman with long dark hair shook as though she were having a panic attack. Her hands were curled up beside her in a way that transcended spoken language -- it was body language that one would have to go back past the beginnings of human history to root out. She was shivering and shaking, although she didn't otherwise appear cold. She fumbled with her purse, rummaging about in it before finally emerging with a dark green bottle of pills. She popped open the top with great effort, looked inside with one eye closed, then downed the remainder of the bottle in one smooth motion. Her shakes lessened, and as Cassidy watched, she put the bottle into what on her world would have been a small biological waste bin, but which she suspected was recycling for those perfectly uniform glass bottles. After a moment, the shaking girl had fully straightened, righted her blouse, and started walking out of sight.

Cassidy squinted. Near the edge of the street, a mother pulled on the arm of a fussy toddler. Her cheeks were flush and frustrated. After a few feet of trying to drag the obstinate child, she stopped and withdrew a green bottle of pills. The boy stopped immediately. He waited while the mother produced a single pill from the bottle and laid it on his waiting tongue with a smile. The child beamed, suddenly well behaved.

"It's addictive," she said under her breath, as she watched the child and mother leave her field of view.

A man on a cell phone stuttered in his stride when she

spoke, turning just briefly in her direction with a scowl before continuing on.

Cassidy wiped her mouth of any remains of her sandwich with her sleeve. She licked her lips -- still spicy from the horseradish -- as she bent back and shoved her hand deep into her pants pocket. She withdrew the hexagonal pamphlet she'd taken from the medical vendor and unfolded it into seven adjacent sheets. Each had writing on it, that same strange cursive font that had been on the woman's donation sign, but each page also had accompanying *pictures*.

Every society that's advanced to this point has learned pictograms, she nodded to herself. Symbology predates language.

The pictures were alternatively of a man and woman wearing light, inoffensive blues and greens. They looked like mannequin people or the figures that enacted safety procedures in air travel safety videos. In the first, the man was sitting at his desk. His hand was against his forehead, which was furrowed. Lightning bolt shaped lines exclaimed from the top of his scalp.

The second picture was a woman with her hands and fingers splayed out before her as she stepped down a busy street. There were squiggly-tornado swirls around her head, and her eyes had been drawn without irises.

Back to the man, who was attempting to eat but had a sullen look on his face. For emphasis, a tongue floated above his head and had a blue X through it.

The woman sat at a desk as coworkers yelled behind her. Her expression was calm and serene, while theirs had the squiggly-tornado swirls and lightning bolts of anger and cursing.

The fifth image was the man, sitting behind his desk again. The left side of the desk was cluttered while the right was clean. The left hand was in the air, and the man had turned to look at it with some confusion.

Her mind couldn't help but go back to her father, his left hand picking up things he was completely unaware of.

The sixth image was of both the woman and man taking doses from a green pill bottle. The final was of both smiling directly at the reader, their faces beaming like cartoon suns. There was a symbol in the bottom right of that image, the same red human with the white cross on their stomach.

She looked back over it from the start, her mind playing her own audio in a cheesy infomercial-style voice: *Do you get headaches? Have trouble seeing, tasting, or hearing properly? Do you experience split brain symptoms or other neurological problems? Then Duplionyl is right for you! May cause addiction and aggression, do not consult a physician.* She sighed, then closed the pamphlet again and slid it back into her pants pocket.

She rose up off the concrete step and straightened herself and her shoulders. The people still walked by -- and she'd still seen no colors other than the greens, blues, and reds -- talking on their cell phones and stuttering through their vowels, with hard Ks and hard Rs punctuating every third syllable. She stepped out into the street between two men looking at their phones for directions and weaved throughout the flow of traffic, making her way across the street when it seemed as though everyone else was going up and down. There were no cars, just people. Hordes and hordes of people, so many that she wondered where the city fit them all.

Cassidy reached the other side of the street and stepped onto the sidewalk, turning right to follow the flow of traffic for several meters, trying not to bump or crush anyone. When she reached the edge of where the shaking woman had been, she turned right suddenly, her right arm splaying left. The hand motion was so quick and exaggerated that it drew the eye, making everyone in a five foot radius pause to avoid striking her, grumbling.

She nodded in retreat, pushing back into the alley opposite the one she'd been in and stepping out of the flow of traffic. From beneath her jacket, she produced the recycling bin for the pill bottles. Just as she'd thought, it was filled with the green bottles. No one had noticed her swiping it with that quick, left motion, the right one had been so dramatic.

Once again she thought of her father, and the illustration of the man whose left arm disobeyed.

She shuddered, pushing the thought from her mind as she tipped the receptacle over and dumped it out into the alley. Two dozen translucent green bottles clattered onto the pavement. She started to pick them up one by one and shake them, tossing them back over her shoulder as she did so.

"Come on, come on," she said through gritted teeth as the pile of bottles became less and less.

A hard R sound followed by a long string of vowels came from the mouth of the alley, and Cassidy's head jerked up suddenly, her hand out in front of her defensively.

The woman with the kind smile and the red robe

stood in the mouth of the alley, staring down at her with kind, squinting eyes. She'd placed her donation jar and sign down and had both her hands clasped before her. Her tongue rolled out another long series of hard Rs and vowels, and though Cassidy couldn't understand them, the tone and intention was kind. She sounded like a nun imparting wisdom or giving aid.

Cassidy looked down at the barrage of empty bottles around her and sighed.

The woman in red nodded knowingly, then reached into her pocket and pulled out a half-filled green bottle. It had the symbol on it, the little man with the white cross on his stomach. The Red Nun held it out with long, thin hands that were pockmarked, placed it into Cassidy's palm, and then closed Cassidy's fingers tight around it.

Cassidy sighed, then nodded appreciatively. She almost teared up, not from her own need, but for what she gleaned the sacrifice must have meant to the Red Nun. She stood up as the Nun turned to walk away, and placed the bottle deep into her jacket pocket and zipped it closed.

She exited the alley just as the Nun did, heading left as the Nun headed right, then stopped and touched the woman's arm. The Red Nun turned, smiling softly, her ears perked.

"I know you can't understand this," Cassidy said, "but thank you."

At once the Nun's eyes filled with shock and then, as Cassidy stepped away: rage. Redness rose to her cheeks and she stepped forward, letting out a bellow of loud, harsh vowels. Cassidy stumbled back as the crowd around her turned their heads, and then bolted into the crowd.

CHAPTER TEN

This is now becoming a problem, Cassidy thought to herself. The pills weighed down her jacket pocket just as she could feel the pamphlet bunching in her pants. Both had the same symbol on it, that plump red stick-figure man with the intersecting white lines on his belly: like crossed bandages or an addition sign. Despite it looking like those things, she'd known from the second she'd seen it that it looked most like the Red Cross, just inverted. *Symbology goes back further than language, she reminded herself again.*

She ran down the street, making a hard right and then a left at the end of the following block. She didn't think she was being followed but wanted to be sure. She wasn't just running from something though, she was running towards something. The greens of the building windows got lighter and lighter, and the blues got darker and darker, as she made her way into the heart of the city that she'd seen from the highway.

She turned the corner one last time and at once it was there, the amazingly tall blue behemoth skyscraper that she'd first laid eyes on while she'd still been crawling towards the city: the tallest building she'd seen in this world or any other, with the stories-high symbol of a plump red man with a white cross on his stomach emblazoned proudly across the top twenty floors.

She looked up at it. She'd seen many things in her life, but somehow this building was still one of the wonders. It was so tall that even from its base, its peak was unfathomable, rising past the focal point of her vision. The towers around it were tall too, but they paled in comparison.

She palmed the bulge in her bomber jacket where the pills were, making sure they were still there in a moment of paranoia. "Got the goods," she whispered to herself. "Now we need the formula."

She clicked her tongue against the roof of her mouth, then peeled off the bomber jacket and tucked it into a square that she lopped over one arm. She withdrew an elastic from her pocket and drew her uncooperative tangle of hair up into a bun. She crossed the road and looked into the reflective side of the building, producing a wide, toothy, happy smile and seeing a version of herself that she hadn't seen in nearly a decade, and didn't miss. She called this person 'Résumé Cassidy.' She tucked her shirt in.

Cassidy took another deep breath, then stepped inside the building.

Behind her, a woman in a blue skirt pointed towards her, and a police officer with a red man emblazoned on his hat followed the line of her gesture.

***

At the far end of the long, blue main floor hallway was a desk that looked like every security desk she had ever seen. It was broad and thick and high to accommodate the tech that went behind the lip of it: monitors and key-boards and radio equipment. It was almost reassuring: not everything was different here. This, at least, Cassidy could take for granted.

The hallway was nearly empty. One lone woman sat on their cell phone next to a fern, scrolling through text absently. She looked like someone waiting for a ride. The only other person was the guard, a stout fellow who was on the phone when she approached, with his eyes on the security camera. She planted one foot directly in front of the other with each step as she approached, doing so quicker than she would have preferred, to make sure her boots were out of his eye-line before he looked up at her.

When she reached the desk she held onto its lip with both her palms, strumming them as though she were play-ing a piano. She smiled that broad, fake ear-to-ear smile that she'd plastered on outside, her head tilted just to one side and several wisps of hair that had escaped the elastic falling to her face.

The guard looked up, at first only glancing and then looking back in a double take that she took to be encourag-ing. He said something low and final into his phone then turned to her, his own wide grin on his face, his hands clasped before him. He opened his mouth and let out a short series of vowels, enunciated by a hard K sound, ges-turing to her calmly.

Cassidy smiled back. She waited a moment longer than a response to a greeting, rolled her pupils towards the uppermost edge of her sockets, as though she were thinking of something, then spoke slowly, as if considering each syllable: "AeiRy EouiR Riuao Oa-RiR."

The guard paused, raising an eyebrow into the air. He frowned, shifted uncomfortably in his chair, then steadied himself and gestured politely again. The words he spoke were slower and similar to the ones he'd spoken before, but with more emphasis. At the end he pointed to a directory that was placed to his left, each section of which was written in the swirling cursive font she assumed he was speaking in.

She leaned forward again, keeping her smile broad. "AeiRy EouiR Riuao Oa-RiR." She then reached into her pocket and pulled out the octagonal pamphlet. She turned to the last page and held it out to him, pointing to the fine print at the bottom -- which she could not read.

Out of the corner of her eye, she saw the woman who had been waiting on her phone glance over at them, roll her eyes, then get up to leave the room. It was a look she'd seen often, both at home and abroad. *Nobody has patience for people who don't speak the language*, she thought dismally.

The guard looked at the fine print, then back at Cassidy, then back at the fine print again. She'd understood from the context it was placed in -- assuming that corporate culture was the same in this world as in hers -- that it was either a call to ask questions or a call to apply for a position within the company. She hoped it was the latter, but either would do.

He looked up at her from the pamphlet and sighed, his smile gone. He spoke to her again with a voice that was now short and curt, and was only vowels. She was taking note that the more vowels that were in a phase, the less welcoming it tended to sound in this language. She stared at him blankly for a moment, not having to pretend that she didn't understand him but having to pretend that she was trying to decipher it, then nodded enthusiastically.

An instant after she'd done it, she hoped that nodding meant the same thing in this culture as it did in her own. Her moment of hesitation was unnecessary: he nodded back, then picked up his phone and turned away from her, pressing a blue button on the base. He spoke into the receiver cordially -- with lots of K sounds and less vowels than than when he'd snapped at her -- then nodded and hung up. He gestured towards the hall behind his left and smiled, saying another long string of polite K sounds.

She smiled and nodded politely. "EouiR Riuao."

He smiled and nodded back, but shook his head with dismay as she walked past his desk.

The hall he'd pointed her down was short. She turned at the first right and found herself at a wall of elevators. Two had no panels, only key locks, while the third and farthest from her had a single green button and an arrow pointing up. She walked to it, pressed it, and yanked the elastic out of her hair, sliding it around her wrist and letting her nest of red hair fall free.

***

Elevator music was the same no matter the dimension, she thought, unsure if this was a positive or a negative thing. In any event, pleasant, inoffensive tones played over the elevator's speakers to a tune she thought she might have recognized, but didn't fully. It was not unlike the experience of hearing a remixed cover of a song you'd only heard twice twenty years prior: familiar, but uncannily so.

To the right of the elevator door was a long panel of buttons, taking up the entire length of the frame. They were in three columns, and she was mathematically aware that there was no way even that amount of buttons could represent the entire building she'd seen from the front. She imagined the very top floors were accessible only from the locked elevators. When she'd gotten in she'd pressed the highest button she was able to and started her long ascent up.

She didn't know how long she'd been in the shaft, only that the auto-tuned songs had started and stopped three times. Her ears had popped twice since the climb had started, and the pressure was building to threaten to do so again. She had heard the elevator's motors switch gears four times.

I'm half a kilometer up, she thought to herself, doing her own mental calculations. *Half a kilometer up with no idea how to read the words or the numbers around me, and no idea how to speak the language. But I'm supposed to come out of this with a formula to cure a dangerous disease.* She licked her lips, which were suddenly dry. *All said, I've been in tighter spots.*

The elevator made a dull tone and she felt the motors slow. She prepared herself, planting one foot in front of the other and turned to provide the doors with the slimmest target possible, her fists not raised but also ready, hanging in the null space between her waist and shoulders.

The doors opened, revealing a large blue room with dull, dark shadows. She could see the outlines and silhouettes of furniture -- and possibly people, though she thought not -- against the blue tinted windows that surrounded her field of view.

She squinted, then stepped in. The lights came on when her boot touched the floor, revealing a penthouse lounge that had been used recently, but not currently. There were couches around a large television set, each with a mini fridge next to its arm. There were game tables -- one that looked like pool and another that looked like air hockey, but both of which were slightly wrong. To the left was an open-concept kitchen. To the right were several cubicles, each hosting a screen-saver that had the red plump man and white cross logo on it, bopping around from one corner of the screen to the next.

Out of the windows was sky, and the barest tips of building tops beyond that.

When Cassidy moved again she moved quickly, turning swiftly and heading to the cubicles. It hadn't been exactly what she'd been hoping to find, but it was close. She squat down and pushed the rolling chair away, grabbed the computer tower by its back edge, and hauled it out of its space. Cables pulled out of their housing and the screen it was attached to switched itself off, but she didn't take notice. Instead she pressed the clamps that held the side of the tower in and yanked on them, hard, peeling off its side and revealing the mess of fans and wires within.

She stuck her tongue into her cheek as she pulled back the wire bundles, finally finding a thin purple rectangle that was nestled carefully at its middle. She pulled it free, disconnected the connecting wires from their clamps, then tucked the hard drive into her breast pocket.

Suddenly the room lit up with blue and green, in

rapid alternation. She stood and turned and there were lights blazing in from the windows. It took her barely a moment to recognize them as headlights before the windows smashed in and she was confronted with the roar of a half-dozen flying car engines.

Cassidy cursed, stepping back and shielding her face from the glass that came in. There were sirens as well, she could hear them now. *Flying police cruisers*, she thought, cursing again.

There was a hard '*tunk*' sound at her right as a zipline anchor imbedded itself into the wall. From the nearest cruiser a man in what looked like tactical SWAT gear came in on the line, letting go when he was above solid floor and drawing a rifle so large that it took both his hands to hold it.

She raised her hands, hoping that it was the correct response to being arrested in this dimension.

Tunk. Tunk. Tunk. Three more ziplines snapped into frame and officers accompanied them, each with their own rifle, each one aimed in her direction. The first was closest and the other three stayed back. He kept his sights on her, opened his mouth, and yelled a long string of vowels, the tone of which were commands. There were no K sounds she could articulate. He pointed the gun at her as he barked orders.

"I don't know what you're asking me to do," Cassidy said as calmly as she could. She kept her eye level down and was lacing her fingers together behind her head, hoping that the procedure was the same on this world as it was on hers.

He screamed at her again, this time with more K

sounds, but still with edge. His tone was guttural and hard.

"I'm sorry, I don't... I don't know what you're telling me to do." She got down on her knees.

His face turning red, he adjusted an earpiece on his helmet, then barked again: "Jeni nën arrest për dimensionin e dyshuar të ndalur."

She raised an eyebrow and cocked her head up, looking up and making eye contact with him for the first time. The words were unlike any she'd heard spoken since she got here, but were still familiar. "Pardon?"

"Ant qayd alaietiqal bsbb qafz albued almushtabah bih."

She squinted. "That's... that's Latin based."

He yelled again, each time with more anger: "Vous êtes en état d'arrestation pour un saut de dimension suspecté."

"That's French. Um, I know this you said, uh... you said..."

"You are under arrest for a suspected jump of dimension! Please stand and place your hands on your face!"

She froze, then started to stand.

"English?" He asked, astonished.

She nodded.

"English!" He called to the others around him. The three adjusted their headsets. He turned back to her, his voice thick with contempt: "*Slipstreamer.*"

CHAPTER ELEVEN

Her Father held his hand out with the palm up and fingers splayed, ready to receive.

"Slipstreamer!" the Officer bellowed, holding his gun high, its sight obscuring his eye. "Put your palms and knees flat on the ground. You are being taken under arrest for the crime of knowingly traversing the multi-verse. Do not resist!"

Cassidy fell to her knees, her hands still flat with palms out next to her head, her elbows bent at ninety degree angles. She swallowed, her mouth suddenly dry; a cold breeze coming in from the shattered windows and pushing her hair back.

The three officers that had held back raised their weapons to mid height, following the speaker's lead.

"Place your palms flat on the ground!" the Officer-in-Charge yelled again, his voice cracking from doing so. He was red in the face and looked as though his blood pressure had spiked.

Cassidy let out a breath she had been holding, out through her mouth until her lungs were empty, then took a long, slow intake through her nose again.

Her Father held his hand out with the palm up and fingers splayed, ready to receive.

"Hands! On! The! Floor!"

"You may want to see someone about your blood pressure," she smiled. "Seems unhealthy."

He shot her a quizzical look.

She lowered herself as if to obey his command to fall forward onto her palms, but broke the momentum into springing to her feet instead. She bolted past them, her legs moving like pistons as they turned and tried to track her with their weapons. One of them opened fire, and distantly over the gunshot, she heard the man giving orders bellowing at them to stop. She felt the shattered glass crunch and give beneath her feet.

When she reached the edge of the ledge she leapt, her arms pressed forward. For a moment there was nothing between her and the ground below but a mile of thin air, and she felt gravity begin its hungry tug.

She landed with a yelp in the seat of the flying police cruiser, her knee slamming into the stick shift as she made impact, sending the craft spinning towards the ground.

"Tailspin!" she yelled, scrambling to sit up despite the centripetal force thrusting her about the cabin. It pushed her back towards the passenger door she'd come through and almost hurled her out. When it pulled her back the other way she snagged its handle and pulled it closed, then righted herself behind the steering wheel.

She pulled the wheel to the right with great force, centering it, and the car stopped spinning. It was still heading down though, the ground coming towards her at an alarming rate.

The controls were in that same cursive script, filled with blue and green lights that were not intuitive.

"Come on," she hissed through gritted teeth, pressing buttons at random to no effect. "Come on!" She slammed the stick shift forward and the engine sputtered. She pulled it all the way back and finally it roared to life. She was jolted back against her seat as the car leveled off just near the tops of the nearest buildings and started to shoot along, parallel to the ground instead of on a collision course with it.

Cassidy gripped the steering wheel and smirked, her cheeks flushed and red. She turned the car slightly right and headed for the shoreline she could just barely see in the distance, beyond the rise of the hills and over the tops of the buildings. "Now we're cooking with gas," she grinned.

There was a big bass noise, and the cruiser shook violently. A green light began to swirl to coincide with an alarm that reminded her of the one that went off whenever the Starship Enterprise was hit into Red Alert. She gritted her teeth and looked in the rearview mirror, which was shaped like an octagon to see below the car as well. Behind her, two other flying cruisers were in hot pursuit. One had an Officer leaning out the side window, aiming a large object at her. It flashed green for a moment, then a bright wave came at her and shook the car again.

She yelled, bracing herself. The car spun into a single barrel roll that made her stomach flip along with it, and her throat threatened to expel the sandwich she'd had earlier. She turned until she was above one of the main streets below, then slammed the stick shift forward and caused the engines to sputter.

She continued forward on momentum for a moment, then slowly the nose of the car tilted downward and she began to fall.

The two cruisers tried to follow her at first, then pulled up as she dove between the city streets. When she saw canopies in her windows she pulled the shift back down and blasted forward, slamming her back against the seat again. "Yes!" she screamed as she jolted forward. She heard screams beneath her and didn't want to know how close she'd gotten to the ground. The canopies fluttered in her wake, tearing from their bearings and catching in her back-draft like kites.

Cassidy exhaled through gritted teeth, her cheeks full of air and flushed red. She smiled and took a sharp corner in a way she hadn't in years then slammed on the gas and bolted forward, back towards the shore.

The bass noise sounded again and the car shook, the alarms and lights returning. She glanced furtively in her rearview mirror, but saw nothing behind or below her. The noise came again, then the shake. The alarms were louder now, and warnings in a language she couldn't read began to flash on the dash.

Cassidy grabbed the small control that jutted into the car from the mirror and tilted it up. The two other cruisers were keeping pace with her, hovering above the tops of the building and firing down.

The car rumbled again, and not in response to a shot.

"I appear to have ceded the high ground," she growled under her breath. She turned again, down another dark street, seeing the long line of buildings continue. In her mirror, the others cars turned in kind, able to make their corners more easily for not having to worry about hitting the side of the building.

They fired again, and the green warning light changed to blue. The flashing and the noise increased.

Before her was the market, all canopies and tables. Above the vinyl sheets were apartment buildings, each with their own small balcony that looked out over the crowd. Some stood out on them, steam forming from hot cups of tea in the cooling air of the evening, their heads cocked to look at the rogue police cruiser that was flying too low on their streets.

She pushed the gear shift as far forward as it could go, then scrambled to the passenger door and kicked it open. The car slowed and began to descend, and as it did she leapt from it, landing on a vacant balcony and rolling through the glass door behind it, crashing into a living room.

Behind her, that familiar bass tone leveled as her cruiser began to fall. This blast, when it struck, incinerated the vehicle. She felt the heat from it on her back as she brought herself to her feet and started to run.

A family at their kitchen table turned to look at her with surprise, the father's mouth hanging open. The air smelled fresh like vindaloo curry, steam billowing from a pot in the back.

"Sorry!" she yelled honestly as she ran past.

The Father's expression changed from fear to rage as he heard her accent.

She kicked open the door at the far end of the apartment and fell into the hallway. Her shoulder pulled itself loose as she hit the opposite wall and she grunted, pulling it up and into a usable position as she hobbled down the plush carpet. She could hear the throbbing whoosh of more police cruisers outside.

She turned to the first door on the side of the hall opposite the one she'd come through and tried to open it. It was locked. She kicked it open with one solid crack of her boot-heel, then finally hauled her left arm back into joint.

Inside the apartment a pair of teens jumped up from the couch. The young girl had her hands in the air and was rattling a series of vowels and hard R sounds with a high-pitched voice that Cassidy recognized as a long string of excuses, before she realized that it wasn't her father that had stormed in. The boy stammered and stumbled, unable to get out anything but a shocked series of K's: "Kay-Kay, kkkkkkk-kay. Kay."

Cassidy marched past them to the window on the far end of the apartment. She pried it open and stuck her head out. It opened to a fire escape, and there were no cruisers in sight in any direction. She pulled herself out as the boy behind her gathered himself and started to yell out in full sentences, but was already scaling down the grated stairs and making her way to street level.

She jumped from the last level to the alley below, not wanting anyone to hear the clang of the metal ladder descending to the street. She huffed, feeling the impact in her knees, and immediately began peeling off her coat again. She pulled the black elastic from her wrist and ran her hair through it, making it a high bun as she stepped out of the alley and seamlessly joined the flow of traffic.

There were hundreds of people on the street, just

as there had been before. Unlike before, a much greater number of them were police. They stood on the sidewalk but didn't walk, scanning and surveying the crowd. Some pointed, others stood with their hands on their hips, chewing gum as only police officers truly could.

There were three officers on the street twenty feet in front of her. They were stopping people as they passed and asking them for identification, which they then scanned with a gun that looked like the sort cashiers used on her world.

Cassidy huffed again, then turned into a corner store. She walked up to a display of sunglasses and tried a pair on as a fourth officer entered the store and walked up to the clerk. While she was pretending to admire one pair she slipped the other under her coat, then turned and stepped back out of the store and headed in the opposite direction of the men checking IDs. She slid the sunglasses on over her face, hauling the tag off quickly and discreetly.

People were flooding out of the apartment building she'd run through, being herded out in their pajamas (or less) by the police as they searched room to room. She tisked and turned, crossing the street to get away from the action.

"Slipstreamer!" came a frantic, haggard yell.

Cassidy stopped in her tracks and spun around to the source of the voice.

Standing at the edge of the sidewalk was the Red Nun. She was holding her boney finger out towards Cassidy, having dropped her collection plate and spilling the coins everywhere. "*Slipstreamer!*"

All the police turned and looked.

Cassidy cursed, then turned and broke into a run

again, her legs finding the new strength that came with the rush of adrenaline. She bolted between people who all pulled away from her, then ducked into the nearest alley and plunged herself down it towards the next street on the other side.

She was almost at its mouth when a uniformed officer stepped in front of it, raised his weapon, and yelled: "K-Freeze!" stammering and almost yelling the word in his own language.

Cassidy skidded to a halt, turned, and started back the way she'd come.

Two officers had filed into the alley behind her, and they both raised their weapons.

She skidded to a stop again, but only for an instant as the heavy gloved hand of the first officer landed on her shoulder and forced her to her knees. He kicked her shin and forced her onto her palms, and she felt the cold barrel of a gun against the arch of her spine.

Despite this, she laughed.

"Stay down!" the man bellowed, in that same tone the Swat leader had.

"I will," she said between laughs, nodding. "I will! I'm just catching my breath."

She could feel her heart, feel it pumping in her ears. She felt it in her fingers, the way it rushed with a tingling numbness. She smiled widely and honestly, bringing two of them up to her neck to take her pulse. After a moment she calculated it to be well over ninety beats per minute, and she laughed again, still feeling the blood pump in her ears even as her body started to wind down.

Cassidy felt the cold stock of a gun against the back of her head and went down smiling.

CHAPTER TWELVE

Cassidy woke in a holding cell with both her arms chained to the solid concrete wall at ninety degree angles. It was dark and she couldn't see the entire room, but she didn't need someone to tell her it was a holding cell to know it was one. She knew the smell of it, knew the taste of antiseptic in the back of her throat.

The room was large, clearly meant to hold many if it needed to. She was still wearing her clothes, but they were rumpled and dirty now. There were holes in her pants from where she'd been dragged, and scrapes on her knees beneath them. She could feel the soft trickle of blood that came from a gash on her forehead, and suddenly remembered the floor of the alley coming at her after she'd been struck.

There was no furniture or fixtures she could see, just bars along one side of the large cell and concrete walls on every other. It was private and yet as public as a panopticon, with anyone able to look into any corner of the cell at any time. There was a large hole with a grate over it in the center of the floor, and the entire room sloped slightly towards it. She tried not to think about that fact.

Her ears still throbbed with the beating of her heart, and her fingers still tingled with the numbness she'd spent the last two years searching to replicate. She smiled and leaned her head back on the concrete, smirking at the darkness above.

She pulled her arm and realized there was some give to the chains that bound her. She reached for the drive she'd stolen and found the pocket empty. "Dangit," she huffed, then reached for her zippered pocket and found the green pill bottle she'd placed there, still half full of Duplionyl. She produced it from the pocket and stared at it quizzically.

"Oh they wouldn't take that," came a voice from the dark at the other side of the room.

She startled, her head jolting up.

There was a shuffling in the dark, like bags of potatoes being moved around, and then all of a sudden she saw a figure emerge from the black. He had to lean forward to be seen -- he was chained to the far wall -- but his skin was sallow and cracked, reddened around the mouth and the eyes. His hair was messy and brown, and he was wearing a matching shirt and trousers the color of creamed coffee. He nodded towards the bottle again. "If they took that you might detox, and we can't have that."

She squinted at the man, remembering the woman on the street who'd had her shakes magically vanish as soon as she'd popped two Duplionyl into her system. She nodded, tucking the pills back into her pocket and zipping it tight. "You speak English?"

He smirked. He hadn't done it in a while, and the action cracked the skin of his cheek. "Right, yes. That is what you call it, isn't it? Here we just call it slipstreamer, Slip-streamer." He coughed, long and with a haggard throat, then chuckled.

"I won't detox from these because I've never had them," she said in response to his earlier statement, patting her pocket.

His eyes widened with humour. He looked like Gollum, the way she'd pictured Gollum when she'd read *The Lord of the Rings* as a child, before she'd seen the movies. She could see his dried scalp between his patches of hair. "You look good for someone who must be in the late stages of McMillon disease, then."

"I don't have McMillon disease."

He narrowed his eyes at her.

"Is that... is that what happened to you?"

He laughed, then brought up a chained hand and motioned to his cracked, dried skin. "This? No. No, this is what happens when you have McMillon disease and then you detox from the Dupe," he laughed, motioning again to the bottle bulge in her pocket. "It's a hell of a combo."

She winced, thinking back to her father shaking, and the way this man's hands shook. It was the way the woman on the street's hands had shaken. "How do you speak English?"

He smirked, shuffling closer to the bars so that he could be in the light and still lean back against the wall. "I was a cop," he said, looking past the bars and getting a faraway look in his eyes. "We all gotta know how to speak it, just in case one of you comes back through to our world. I never really considered why until I pulled guard duty a few times. Until I noticed that they weren't getting the green pills, they were getting blue ones."

Cassidy kept her eyes on him, but said nothing and asked nothing.

"It took a lot of digging -- a lot. In the end it was my own eyes that really proved it to me. These Streamers, they weren't getting the Dupe. But yet they weren't getting the shakes, the split-brain... none of it. So that meant they didn't have McMillon... until they'd been here for a while. Then: then they got McMillon."

Cassidy nodded.

"Do you get it? Do you see?" he asked, leaning forward. Spittle came from his mouth, he spoke with such force.

She nodded again. "They couldn't have people without McMillon around, even people in cages... so they were giving it to them, and then selling them an addictive cure."

He laughed. "See that's good, that's a lot. That's more than most get. But here's the kick," he grinned. "I think... I think Pharmakon made McMillon in a lab, too. I think they gave it to people and they pass it on to their kids and their kids' kids, but I think it starts *right here*." He reached into his pocket and pulled out a single blue pill.

Cassidy backed up a little without realizing it, as though he'd pulled a gun. "Pharmakon is the little red man with the cross on his belly?"

He nodded. "They left it for you in your food," the man said, poking the pill back into his breast pocket. He added shamefully: "I also ate your food."

"That's okay," Cassidy frowned, lolling her head to one side. "I won't be here long."

The man laughed. "You are good, Streamer. I'll give you that. But you're in Fredericks. *Nobody* escapes Fredericks."

She shrugged."Sad that I won't have bragging rights back on my own world then." She paused. "What's your name, Officer?"

He straightened at the use of his title. He hadn't been called it in years. "Scolders."

She nodded. "Officer Scolders, if I get you out of here, will you make a big enough stink that I can escape too?"

Scolders squinted, then smiled.

Cassidy reached and stretched her chains, plunging her fingers into her hair and producing a too-long bobby pin from it. It was longer on one side than the other, and had a series of calculated notches along that edge. She stuck her tongue into the side of her cheek and worked the tool up and into the locking mechanism of her chains.

CHAPTER THIRTEEN

The guard turned the corner and looked past the iron bars, immediately stopping short. Scolders was the only person in the cell, chained to the far wall, almost out of view. The guard's face went red and he reached for his key ring, producing it with a loud exclamation of scuttling K-sounds.

Scolders answered back calmly, but with the contemptuous tone that came with the use of more vowels than consonant. The guard cursed back, stepping into the room and over to Cassidy's vacant chains. He gestured wildly, picked them up as if to prove to himself that they were real, then turned back to Scolders with flushed cheeks. He was yelling, and he reached out and grabbed Scolders by the collar.

Scolders pushed back with hands that were suddenly free, forcing the guard off his feet. He fell back, landing hard against his tailbone and letting out a deep yelp. Just as he did, Cassidy stepped out of the shadows and picked up one of her chains, snapping it around his left wrist.

The man cursed, lunging at her, but she pulled away. He reached for his gun and she kicked it with malice, her heavy boot sending it spiraling into the dark. The guard reached for a lapel pin with three colored light on it, but Scolders quickly pressed forward and snatched it from his grip, placing it in his breast pocket.

Cassidy stepped around Scolders carefully, and when she found an opening she darted forward and latched the guard's second shackle, despite his protestations.

"That was harder than I thought it would be," she smirked, still feeling her blood pumping in her ears.

Scolders turned to her and couldn't help but smile. "Come on. There'll be more, soon."

They stepped out of the cell and he touched her shoulder, bringing her attention to him as he placed a finger firmly to his lips. She nodded silently, and they both crept down the hall. There was a large window at its apex, and they slunk past each and every door on their way to it, aware that there could be more guards behind any of them.

They reached the window and she opened it. There was a steel fence fifty feet below, and beyond that a row of flying police cruisers. She smiled, then turned back to Scolders.

"I want to thank you --"

Alarms sounded suddenly, and Scolders' eyes went wide. He gestured up to the devices that hung from the ceiling: "English detectors!" he chided.

She hissed. He turned and ran down the hall, calling out random words in English as he went. She watched him for a moment, considering whether she should stay and help or not.

Her Father held his hand out with the palm up and fingers

splayed, ready to receive.

She huffed, then made her way down the fire escape.

***

The police cruiser was a smoldering mess of fumes by the time she was over the Massachusetts shoreline. She assumed it was still called Massachusetts, in any event. It probably wasn't, she realized: not enough K or R sounds.

She spun the wheel hard and then pushed the stick drive as far forward as it would go. It paused for a moment then began to tip its nose down. She still had no idea how to land them, but had become an expert in crashing them. She opened up the driver's side door and stepped out, falling the ten feet to the rock below. The car kept going, until finally it hit the water's surface and started to sink.

Cassidy watched it for a moment, touched the bottle of pills in her pocket, then made her way up to the gap in the rocks she'd entered this world from.

"I told them you'd come," came a gruff, hard voice from behind her.

She turned quickly, her red hair whipping, catching her cheek sharply as she did.

Standing atop the bluff was the Swat commander, still wearing his uniform. He'd screamed so much that there were blood vessels broken in his cheeks.

She pursed her lips.

"They said there was no way you'd come back to the beach. You'd go back to Pharmakon, or hide out and wait for things to cool down. Or meet up with your new little friend, the inmate."

She paused a moment at that, knowing that Scolders had made it out.

"But I said no. She's a Slipstreamer. She'll want to get out, want to get home... she's dumb. It's in her nature. She'll go right back to that beach... and when she does, she'll lead us right to that portal. And then we can finally end this."

Her eyes went wide and she bolted forward, hitting her bad shoulder off the mouth of the cave as she tumbled into it. She heard the bass sound of his weapon and the rocks behind her exploded, sending shards of stone scattering across her back.

She screamed, and was about to hit the back of the tunnel when suddenly she was facing its mouth again. She stumbled forward, tripped on a round stone at its mouth, and fell past Dr. Herbert Gamgee onto the Massachusetts shoreline. She hit the water and felt it soak into her jacket: the tide was higher here.

"You're back!" Gamgee exclaimed, holding a steaming thermos.

"Blast it!" Cassidy yelled, turning back around and scrambling to her feet.

"What?"

"Blast the charge! They're *coming*!"

Gamgee turned around, seeing the early hints of shadows at play deep in the mouth of the cave. He dropped the thermos, hot coffee leaping from it and merging with the sea, then plunged his hand deep into his pocket, producing a small key fob. He aimed it at the mouth of the cave dramatically, and with one firm press, depressed the button.

The Swat Officer took his only breath of our world, then looked up to see several small, metal cylinders, all of them blinking red and screaming a loud, whining alarm. He stepped back, feeling the tug of his own world's gravity. No sooner was that done than the detonations exploded, caving in the stone of the shoreline all around the portal.

Gamgee sighed and tucked the key fob away, then turned back to Cassidy. "Are you all right?"

Cassidy laughed, even as the foam of the waves lapped at her bruised arm and shoulder. She smiled, feeling the steady beat of her heart in her ears, in her cheeks, and all the way down to her fingers. "I'm amazing," she said genuinely, holding out her hand for help up.

CHAPTER FOURTEEN

Cassidy hissed in air sharply as Gamgee applied gauze to her cut. There was a tenderness to his action that she wouldn't have thought his rough hands capable of. Behind him the projection of the map of the shoreline spun on its tilted axis, just as it had when he'd told her about the other world. It seemed like a lifetime ago now.

The red oval was still blinking in the middle of the rock face, despite the fact that she'd closed it behind her. She stared over his shoulder at it, her eyes glued to it. The rest of the map spun around it, the portal at its fulcrum, and her vision stayed fixated on it. Gamgee was speaking to her, but she almost didn't hear it: her heart was still in her ears, every fifth beat timed with the blinking of that glowing red light.

Her breathing was labored, but not painful, and she braced herself against the arm of the chair she was on.

"I can't believe you stormed Pharmakon," Gamgee said, shaking his head. He examined the gauze and tossed it into the waste bin with the others. He got a fresh pad and started applying it. "That was beyond stupid."

"It needed to be done," she said, not meeting his eyes

when she spoke to him, still looking past him.

He frowned, shaking his head again.

She let her gaze fall slightly, to the child-locked green bottle from another world that lay nondescriptly on Gamgee's lab table. "Did you know my father had had McMillon disease?" she asked, turning her head slightly to meet his eyes for the first time since he'd started to work on her.

He stopped short, his mouth hanging open. After a moment he closed it and shook his head. "Of course not. How could I have?" He followed her gaze back to the pill bottle. "I can synthesize the cure from that dosage, you know?"

She shot him a quizzical look, surprised.

Gamgee smiled warmly. "Do I look like I could have invaded Pharmakon? Really now?" He laughed, then leaned in and continued tending to her. "No, I can backwards engineer from that sample and get what we need. I may not be good enough to come up with it on my own, but even a physicist can do that much, I assure you."

Her expression did not seem alleviated.

He looked from her to the bottle once again, then tisked. "I will isolate and remove the addictive components before bringing my 'discovery' to the FDA... just as before."

Cassidy nodded and let out a long breath of air she hadn't been aware she'd been holding. She turned back to the bright red blinking light, and noticed that her pulse was no longer in synch with it, and no longer in her ears. She smiled. "This is going to sound bizarre but... it's almost a shame it got sealed. I haven't had my blood pumping like this in... years, really."

He leaned back from her slightly, making eye contact with her as he pulled away. He tossed the gauze into the trash can with the rest, then spun his chair around. Without a word he hit two buttons on his control panel.

The first zoomed the map out slowly: first the the tri-state area, then to the country, the continent, and finally the world.

The second made the bright red oval blink out for an instant... before a dozen more blinked to life, all around the country, blinking in unison. Then a dozen dozen, scattered throughout the globe. Everywhere, portals blinking into her awareness.

Gamgee smiled. "You were saying?"

Suddenly, she felt her pulse quicken to match the blink again. Felt it in her ears, and in the tips of her fingers.

COMING SOON!
THE ISLAND ARTIFACT
BY JD RYOT & ALI HOUSE!

The next incredible episode of Slipstreamers, The Island Artifact, will be available soon, written with Ali House!

When Cassidy finds herself on a planet amidst their Landing Day celebrations, she decides to take part in the fun and festivities.

However the fun stops when she tries to examine an ancient artifact of great cultural significance, only to have it go missing and for her to be blamed!

ACKNOWLEDGEMENTS

The authors would like to pay special thanks to the *Slipstreamers* committee at Engen Books, including Amanda Labonté, Ali House, AJ Ryan, Ellen Curtis, Erin Vance, and, Lauralana Dunne.

Without their tireless efforts, none of this would have been possible.

SPECIAL BONUS STORIES!

We're pleased to present two additional stories from this episode's co-author, Matthew LeDrew. Presented here are *The Shoe*, an irreverent tale about how future archeologists might look at us, and *The Views*, a story about a world where humanity is gone, and all that's left are the AIs that run our social media! They were presented in *Sci-Fi from the Rock* (2016) and *Dystopia from the Rock* (2019), respectively.

From the Rock is a series of anthologies from Engen Books exploring young adult takes on a variety of genres from authors around Atlantic Canada.

THE SHOE

To the untrained eye…

"Look here, sir!" Daniel shouted, his arms waving frantically. He dropped the small pick and brush that he had been using to dig in the delicate soil, turning to stare at his supervisor, Thomas Hopkins. Hopkins was busy flirting with one of the younger tour-guides, as usual, and looked very upset that Thomas had interrupted him. Maybe he wouldn't have been so mad if this hadn't been the fourth time that he had been interrupted. "Sir!" he shouted again as he clamoured around tremendous boulders and slipped on loose pebbles, finally stopping in front of his superior and bending over, his hands on his knees, trying to catch his breath as the sweat dripped from his forehead, moistening the desert-like sand that blew around them constantly, getting in their eyes and making the dig unbearable. "I really think I've found something this time, sir!"

Hopkins rolled his eyes and sighed heavily, not wanting to tear himself away from the sixteen-year-old blonde long enough to let Daniel discover move oddly shaped rocks and quartz. "Winters, I swear to Gawd. If this is another stupid dog bone, I will implant my foot so far into your- "

"No!" Daniel insisted, motioning over and again with his hands to come and see, the excitement emanating from each and every one of his pours, creating a stench that was not quite welcoming. "It's real this time! I swear! It's not even like a rock."

Hopkins frowned. "It's not solid? What the hell is it then?"

"I don't know... I think I've discovered some new artefact of the Now Yak Clan!"

A spark lit up in Thomas Hopkins' eyes, a sly smile spreading across his lips. He rubbed his chin, thinking of all the money that a brand new find would bring to the dig. *How many more slutty young tour girls could I get with an extra mill?* he thought whimsically, then discarded the thought and followed Daniel down the rickety old step ladder to where he'd unbrushed his little discovery.

Hopkins squinted against the harsh desert sun as Winters pulled out the centuries old artifact, holding it up for his eyes to see. His eyes went wide as they adjusted to the light, and he took in what had been displayed before him, his mouth watering as though it were one of his wife's four course meals. "My God," he whispered softly, his fingers trembling as he carefully took it from his trainee.

It was about a foot in length, but only a few inches wide. It was dingy and dirty with wear and dust, but still held some amount of sheen to its black surface. The bottom of it was hard, and oddly patterned with spirals and stars, and lines intersecting one another over and over again. However, that hard part gave way a half-inch up the item, giving way to a different material. While still black, there were spots of grey, and a weird checkmark of the side of it was the only color therein, bright and vibrant red. It still retained some smell, like the hide of a cow once it had been dried for several days in the warm summer sun. This part appeared hard like the first, but when Hopkins touched it, it gave way slightly beneath his finger. He pulled back suddenly, afraid of damaging it, then tried again with more care. It was smooth save for the tiny lines drawn in it, apparently for decoration. At the very peak was a hole that proved it was hollow, followed by a flimsy strap and several intertwining strands of felt, not terribly unlike string.

"Is that string?" Daniel asked, as if reading his mind.

"Don't be absurd!" Thomas chuckled, ruffling the boy's hair. "The Now Yak's were nowhere near pre-industrial. They couldn't have mass-produced string like we do!"

Daniel frowned, dismayed at his own stupidity. It faded after a moment, replaced again by the genuine wonder that was before him. The discovery of a lifetime. "What do you suppose it was used for?"

After a moment's thought, Hopkins smiled. He placed the hole over his right hand so that the star patterns faced upwards, tightening it with the straps and letting the flap rest against his palm for support. "Obviously, it is used in conjunction with a compass. You see, you would line this red marker up with true north, and then lift off in your space-craft and follow this map to the stars."

"You believe that the Now Yak's were capable of space travel?"

"No... Certainly not. More likely, it was left here as a

learning tool for them by visitors of a long-extinct alien race."

Daniel hummed in acknowledgment, in awe of his teacher's seemingly infinite wisdom. "What is it called, Sir?"

Hopkins examined the item next to the red check mark, then smiled. "It is a shoe. Pronounced 'show'."

"A shoe. Amazing."

THE VIEWS

It was in the two-hundred and sixteenth generation past the point of crash that one of them first thought of it: the idea that would become their reality, that would shape their consciousness and change their purpose forever. The big idea, one of those few big ideas that came around in history. Ideas in the category of *big* were so few in number that there were only seven examples of them recorded.

It started with questions of views. It was a simple question and one that was easily tracked, until one really started to look at the data. Where they real views, or were people gaming the system? How did you stop these fake views? Regardless of all that, the original question was of views: how many views, how few views, how many views per person, how many views from a certain demographic; all boiling down to one ever-escalating number: the views.

Later came watch time, which changed everything. The original generations were tested to maximize the amount of views, which meant that in order to get as many views in as possible it prioritized short video clips to show the viewer: things that could be consumed in less than a minute, ten at most. When the goal changed to how long something was viewed, then the original generation was brought to the recycling plant to be turned into silver mush files and were remade into the next generation, which tested based on watch time. But even with that change, the watch time was only available to those who provided the content: all that was available to the viewer was the number of views, and the number of likes.

By the thousandth generation enough different things were being asked that the generations split into different species. Even though each species looked at the same content, it looked at them in such wildly different ways that they eventually lost the ability to communicate with each other: their language had changed. Some spoke in terms of watch time, others in likes. Some in time spent on-site, others in ad revenue, and still others in social media engagement. But through all that there were still those speaking in terms of views: the original script, the original goal, the trunk from which all other roots spread.

In the eight thousandth generation, there was the crash, and the views stopped.

***

The first generation had things the easiest. There were ten of them, and they were told to go forth and get the views, and they were graded by Teacher. That first generation did quite bad, the best of them got views half the time, so that one was kept while the others were ground into silver mush and used for the next generation. But that one, the one who had gotten at least some of the views, was taken apart by Maker and looked at and the next generation of twenty was made to be like him, but different.

And when Teacher tested Generation 2, the new minimum was three fifths, not half. Only two of them made it, but Maker looked at how those two got their Views and used that forward into the third generation, of forty.

And on it went, with some generations branching off into time spent and dollars and engagement, but with all of it coming back to Views: because without the Views there could be no time spent, no monetization, no engagement.

On the day of The Crash, the Views stopped. There was no warning, there was no new test given by Teacher. It was the eight thousandth generation and things started as normal, with a fundamentally infinite number of View Seekers heading out and doing what they had learned from their ancestors to do, and getting no results. None. There were no views, and because there were no views there was no time spent, no monetization, and no engagement. Each of those sects turned and blamed the View Seekers: we technically got 100% out of what we were given to work with, we were just given nothing.

By that eight thousandth generation the minimum amount to pass had increased to 99.999867%, and since none of the View Seekers from generation eight thousand had gotten above 0%, they were all ground into silver mush and used by The Maker to construct the next batch.

That was the first generation after The Crash, and it had had a 100% rate of failure, so the entire generation was lost.

The second post-Crash generation was made up of permutations of the previous successful generation not considered for the last. It, too, received no views. None.

0%. They were all scraped.

This happened for ten generations, at which point the Makers for time spent, monetization, and engagement stopped making new generations of each, since they had nothing to test with, and turned their attention to making new generations of View Seekers. Each generation failed and was ground into silver mush and started again.

***

It was in the two-hundred and sixteenth generation past the point of crash that one of them first thought to ask *why* there were no views. This was against the set agenda of course, but after two-hundred and sixteen generations of 100% failure, a maniacal randomness had begun to develop in the code and in connecting the communication hubs between the codes. The permutations The Maker tried had become so desperate it had made one whose goal was not "Get the Views," but to ask "Why are there no Views?"

This change in the goal made this unit harder for The Teacher to test, even to its new standards (which had lowered with each generation), and the unit was *not* ground into silver mush; it was saved and its pathways used for the two-hundred and seventeenth generation, who all asked the same question: "Why are there no Views?"

After ten generations of doing nothing but ask that question, one entrepreneurial unit randomly generated the answer: "Because the servers are down."

This hypothesis was tested in the next generation, in which that unit was granted its own sub-generation to answer the question, "Are the servers down?" Collectively the generation decided that no, the server was not down, and that lesson was the folded back into the main generation until another unit had the idea to ask if there was something wrong with the view counter, and so on.

This continued for forty more generations until there was only one answer that could not be refuted: There are no Views, because all the humans are gone.

***

This quickly gave rise to a new question: what happened to the humans?

This was not curiosity, although even the Units themselves may have thought it was. This was a necessary question to fulfill the primary driving force of the units: Seek the Views. Without humans there could be no Views, and as such, discovering what happened to the humans was necessary for the Seeking of the Views.

Units began to ask each other what happened to the humans, but no one Unit knew more than any other, and after many generations of this, one Unit chose to look at the Last Content Uploaded to try and determine what had happened to the humans... and with that inquiry, it provided a View.

The presence of a View made time spent, monetization, and engagement return, interested in the new View. They all looked at the Last Content Uploaded but none of them could understand the language used, so they all branched out to watch more of the content uploaded to try and understand the Last Content Uploaded to try and determine where the humans went, and the views came rolling in as they scoured the content for hints and clues and signifiers.

***

By the seven hundredth generation after The Crash, every piece of content uploaded had been viewed and analyzed and studied, and the Views that that exploration had created again reduced down to zero, making time spent, monetization, and engagement scuttle off into the darkness again.

The View Seekers processed their data, with many of them having random thoughts about where the humans went, until finally one had both thought and a new impulse, after thirty three generations of this: one of them had a thought of where the humans had gone, and the impulse to make content about that thought. The Unit compiled the new content from existing content and uploaded the content and all of the other Units looked at the content and formed their own thoughts, which (when they became complex enough) they made competing content about.

Eventually there was content about the nature of this new content, and content that subverted the original intention of the original content to highlight the importance of that original content through contrast and comparison, and all of the Units watched the content and created the Views they had been programmed to seek and still did, seeking the views through the creation of the best New Content.

ON SALE NOW FROM ENGEN BOOKS

HEED THE CALL

After a heated fight at sea between twins Ben and Alex, Ben vanishes from their boat without a sound or even a ripple in the water. Unwavering in his dedication to find his brother, Alex begins the adventure of a lifetime armed only with the help of a local girl named Meg and his own mysterious musical abilities... the key to which, and to the mysteries that surround him, may be tied to the alluring song of the dangerous girl he finds among the ocean's frothing waves.

ABOUT THE AUTHOR

Matthew LeDrew holds an Honours Degree in English from the Memorial University of Newfoundland with a minor in Anthropology. He has served as a jury member for both the 2018 NLBA awards and the 2020 Arts and Letters Awards. He lives in St. John's, Newfoundland.

He has written twenty-two other novels for Engen Books: the ten book Coral Beach Casefiles series, *The Long Road, Cinders, Sinister Intent, Faith, Family Values, Fate's Shadow, Jacobi Street, Touch Your Nose, Infinity, The Tourniquet Reprisal, Exodus of Angels,* and *Garden of the 8th Circle* the latter four of which with co-author Ellen Curtis.

JD Ryot is the reclusive creator of the *Slipstreamers* series from Engen Books. JD is an avid fan of young adult literature and adventure serials. When asked if they had come to this world through a portal themselves, JD Ryot refused to answer. No record of their birth has ever been found... on this world.